# Flight #116 Is Down!

## with Related Readings

Glencoe
McGraw-Hill

New York, New York   Columbus, Ohio   Woodland Hills, California   Peoria, Illinois

## Acknowledgments

Grateful acknowledgment is given authors, publishers, photographers, museums, and agents for permission to reprint the following copyrighted material. Every effort has been made to determine copyright owners. In case of any omissions, the Publisher will be pleased to make suitable acknowledgments in future editions.

*Flight #116 Is Down!* by Caroline B. Cooney. Copyright © 1992 by Caroline B. Cooney. Reprinted by permission of Scholastic, Inc. All rights reserved.

"You Go and I'll Stay a While" from *A Night to Remember* by Walter Lord, © 1955 by Walter Lord. Reprinted by permission of Henry Holt and Company, LLC.

"Justin Lebo" from *It's Our World, Too!* by Phillip Hoose. Copyright © 1993 by Phillip Hoose. Reprinted by permission of Little, Brown & Company.

"A Time to Talk" from *The Poetry of Robert Frost* edited by Edward Connery Lathem, © 1969 by Henry Holt and Company. Reprinted by permission of Henry Holt & Co., LLC.

"Teen Run ER" by Rich Johnson is reprinted, with thanks, from ABC News.

"Too Soon a Woman" by Dorothy M. Johnson. Copyright © 1953 by Dorothy M. Johnson. Reprinted with the permission of McIntosh and Otis, Inc.

**Cover Art:** *Airplanes at the Hong Kong Airport*, 1963, Franklin McMahon. CORBIS.

**NOTE:** *This novel depicts an airline disaster and the ensuing rescue operation. Some situations may be too intense for some readers.*

*Glencoe/McGraw-Hill*

*A Division of The* **McGraw·Hill** *Companies*

Send all inquiries to:
**Glencoe/McGraw-Hill**
8787 Orion Place
Columbus, OH 43240

ISBN 0-07-828262-4
Printed in the United States of America
3 4 5 6 7 8 9 026 04 03

# Contents

## Flight #116 Is Down!

*Continued*

Contents *Continued*

## Related Readings                                                    129

# Flight #116 Is Down!

Caroline B. Cooney

# One

*Saturday:* 5:05 P.M.

The coffee shop was open from six A.M. until midnight. It sat in the middle of nowhere between a video rental shop and a gas station whose pumps were difficult to find behind the row of cars to be repaired, or beyond repair.

Patrick loved the coffee shop. Everybody went there, all the men he admired and wanted to be exactly like.

It had had a lot of names: it had been Joanie's, and The Doughnut Hole, and The Welcome Home, and The Diner on the Hill, until nobody could remember which name fit when, and now it was not called by name at all, but by liquid, as in "I'm going for coffee. Meet me?"

Patrick did not like coffee and wished he could order a Pepsi. But he was learning how to gag coffee down. His original plan was to drink it black because he liked guys who straddled the stools at the counter and said, "Black"—tough and hard, as if saying, "Assassinate Me." But black coffee was disgusting; you might as well drink concentrated river pollution. Then he tried his father's style, "Half a sugar, drop of milk," but that just turned the pollution paler. He was up to "Two sugars, heavy on the milk" now, and he still couldn't figure out why people wanted to pour this stuff into their systems.

But he loved the coffee shop.

Constables, state police, firemen, and ambulance volunteers hung out here. Construction workers, the town crew, state forest rangers—everybody interesting. It often seemed they did nothing but drink coffee; or perhaps drank in shifts, so as to have one person on the job and one swilling coffee. This was where the stories were. How that stupid jerk Masey wired the O'Fallin house so bad that it caused the fire last month, and here summer people were still hiring Masey to do their wiring. How the Stoeckle brothers had probably set their own restaurant on fire for the insurance but looked now as if they'd get away with it. How McCandless's son had married that Epson girl, and that's how he got the job building the addition to the Town Hall, because the Epsons ran everything.

Patrick lived for that kind of gossip.

His geography of Europe and Africa might be a little skimpy, but his geographical knowledge of Nearing River was flawless. Patrick was convinced that he knew every road, every driveway, every shortcut, and the grade of every hill. He knew who ran the snowplows and who did 24-hour tows. He thirsted for more facts about his town, absorbing them for the moment when he called the shots and saved the lives and houses.

Patrick was a Junior on the Ambulance.

He hated this term. It implied stupidity, youth, and a small body. Patrick was smart, seventeen, and weighted in at one eighty. He was a trained and certified EMT: Emergency Medical Technician.

Meanwhile, however, he was also a Junior. Ellington and Darien, Connecticut, also used Juniors for emergency response, but in those towns they were called Explorers. Patrick thought that was even worse than Junior: like, were you going to say to this person having a heart attack, "Oh, just lie down and let me Explore"?

Patrick could take blood pressure, pulse, temperature, and respiration. He could bandage and splint. He could move neck and head injuries. He knew how to control bleeding, treat shock, and deal with belligerent drunks.

Patrick thought it comical that he needed a hall pass to go to the school library—but he could deliver a baby or give CPR without saying Please May I.

The town of Nearing River had no paid medical or fire response; no town in the area ever had. Volunteers handled emergencies. There was one problem. Except for the factory where Patrick's dad worked, there were no jobs in Nearing River. The town—it was stretching things to call Nearing River a town—was pretty remote. People had to drive as far away as Torrington or even Waterbury to get work. Few adults were around by day to volunteer for anything at all.

So the state issued a waiver to Nearing River and allowed sixteen-to eighteen-year-olds to train for ambulance rescue. Juniors on call left high school classes to respond to emergencies. If it weren't for Juniors, it would be very poor planning to have a car accident, a baby, a stabbing, a heart attack, or a drug overdose between eight in the morning and six at night.

Patrick wanted to be a paramedic someday and drive the paramedic's specially equipped Bronco: speeding over curving, ice-slick roads, bringing relief to the wounded.

Actually, most calls were un-wounded. People panicked easily. They called the ambulance for anything. A kid fell off his bike and got three drops of blood on his kneecap and the mother called the ambulance. An elderly woman scraping potatoes scraped her knuckle instead, and she called the ambulance. Two cars ploughed into each other and bystanders called the ambulance when nobody was hurt in the slightest; even the cars weren't hurt.

Patrick had done very little lifesaving.

He tried to be glad that so few local lives were in danger, but deep down he was hoping for a really good catastrophe. Say, an elementary school bus turning over into the ravine on Upper Long Hill.

Then he would catch the thought, stomp on it, swear to God no such horrible idea had passed through his mind; actually glancing upward (Who me, God? Sweet Patrick? Never.) as if to ward off the thunder and lightning he deserved for happily daydreaming of such a thing.

Oh, well, just going to high school was punishment enough. Every day Patrick could not believe they expected him to attend yet again. He studied because his father would kick him out of the house if he didn't, and because his mother was an English teacher who would be ashamed if her son failed.

Patrick adored his parents.

His father was head of maintenance for the only factory in town. Patrick's dad loved his work: always something different—wiring, windowpanes, air-conditioning. The factory had two nice policies: anybody who wanted to donate blood got time off and a company van to take them to the Bloodmobile; and anybody who was a volunteer on Fire or Ambulance could automatically leave for a call.

Rescuing ran in the family.

Patrick's mom had quit driving on the Ambulance Squad after fourteen years of taking one twelve-hour shift a week and now was a dispatcher two nights a week for 911.

Patrick's dad had switched to the Fire Department, having tired of ambulance calls. Stuff like, "HillView Nursing Home, eighty-four-year-old female, difficult breathing" did not whip up Mr. Farquhar's adrenalin anymore. Eighty-four-year-olds in nursing homes were always having difficulty breathing. However, he was now subjected to calls like, "11 Rockrimmon Road, man smells smoke," which, after Mr. Farquhar left work, joined his buddies at the firehouse, yanked out the engines, drove all the way backcountry, would turn out to be a neighbor burning leaves. Mr. Farquhar's enthusiasm for rescue of any kind had hit an all-time low.

Patrick's enthusiasm was at an all-time high. All he needed was somebody to rescue. But regrettably, no matter how Patrick yearned for action, this was basically a very dull part of America. He had to watch television to see a gunfight, a drug war, a volcano, or a forest fire. Even though he loved every inch of Nearing River, it was a mystery to Patrick why anybody lived here. It was so boring.

Yet people were continually moving in.

It amazed Patrick that there were so many people in this small town he did not know. Ambulance call after ambulance call was for a family he had never heard of; a house he had somehow never noticed. Houses lurked behind thick stands of maple trees; driveways sneaked out from behind granite outcroppings; new people moved to town without notifying Patrick. In fact, if he went by the last names of ambulance calls this year, the entire town consisted of sick strangers.

Patrick filled his heavy white coffee mug to the brim with cream, hoping to soften the sewage flavor. It did not. He steeled himself, thinking sadly that men all around the world steeled themselves to face terrorists, civil war, or famine, while he, Patrick, couldn't even swallow coffee.

He took his scanner off his belt and set it on the green plastic counter to admire. He loved his scanner: the black official rectangle, the little red lights zinging around and around the frequencies, ready to stop for any transmission. Tonight, however, the frequencies of state police, local constable (Nearing River didn't even have a police force), and Fire and Ambulance in the three nearest towns remained silent.

Noelle, who ran the diner, and appeared to be the only one on this evening, switched her radio off Easy Listening to the weather channel. Patrick listened skeptically. The weather channel was a joke. It couldn't predict as well as his father could, just walking out the front door. In the last week they had had fog, ice, a dusting of snow, a day of sixty-degree weather, followed immediately by another ice storm. March was Patrick's kind of month; he liked October, too; that was a month you couldn't count on. Months like July, now, or January— they were predictable.

Patrick yearned for something unpredictable; something that would test him; something he could swagger about.

Noelle put Easy Listening back on. Patrick was opposed to the whole concept of Easy Listening. He wanted hard, taxing, tough listening. What was the matter with his life that it just lay around being Easy Listening?

The scanner channels lay silent. The red light flickered from channel to channel without finding any action.

*Saturday:* 5:10 P.M.

The estate was called Dove House.

The mansion had been built a hundred years before by an owner who had been charmed by a dovecote in England when he was abroad. He constructed, therefore, an enormous, shingled, twenty-room mansion for himself and his bride, with tiny windows and tiny dormers below a massive roof. It was ridiculous, out of proportion, and weird—but charming. Anybody arriving for the first time would frown at the house, visibly thinking, What is this thing? Then they would smile, just as visibly thinking, Whatever it is, I kind of like it.

Dove House faced a lovely fieldstone courtyard, complete with fountain. The courtyard entry was European and cozy, while the rear of the Dove House looked out across wide meadows, a deep rock-encrusted ravine, and thick vine-tangled woods. There was a tennis court, a reflecting pond surrounded by roses, and a gazebo.

At one time the owners of Dove House had kept not only doves, but also peacocks and sheep. The Landseths, who had bought the place a dozen or so years before, had been entranced when they inherited this menagerie.

The peacocks, however, had to be abandoned because they were always escaping their enclosure, going off into the woods and shrieking their doomed-child-in-agony shriek. (The neighbors who frantically called 911, the constables and volunteers who set off into the ravines searching for the doomed child, quickly tired of this entertainment.) The sheep were abandoned because they were pretty only from a distance and not close up, but the sheep didn't know that and were always breaking through the fences and getting disgustingly close up. Finally there were only horses, when the

Landseth daughter went through a horsey stage, and fields were cleared and fenced off.

Heidi Landseth had trouble even remembering her horse-crazy years. She'd had two ponies and three horses at one point. Then, when she was twelve, Heidi lost interest. It really had been strange: her life was horse horse horse, and one morning she woke up and didn't care if she ever rode again. Eventually the horses were sold, and now the stable lay empty, and the pony field had to be mowed twice a year to keep it from growing up into woods again.

The lane into Dove House was nearly a half mile long. One vehicle wide, edged by low stone walls, it was romantic and spooky. Branches of overhanging trees formed a tunnel. Rhododendron bloomed purple in the spring, followed by mountain laurel in pale pink. Deer were as plentiful as squirrels.

Heidi loved the drive in any weather: summer, fall, winter, spring. By the gatehouse was a stone bridge that arched like a fairytale illustration, and there the school bus waited for her on Rockrimmon Road. Rockrimmon was also winding and curving, as New England roads are, fitting between glacial boulders and skirting ravines. The school bus tooted to be sure nobody was coming the other way before risking the many blind curves.

There were neighbors, but Heidi and her parents knew few of them; houses here were invisible from the road.

Heidi's parents were the happiest people she knew. They loved their work. Her father was a consultant in international trade with Eastern Europe. Mr. Landseth was always flying to Budapest or Prague and writing up reports in his New York City office. He spoke several languages and sometimes helped the State Department. Her mother was a journalist with a specialty in medicine. If there was a new type of heart surgery in Dallas or an interesting medical phenomenon in San Francisco, Mrs. Landseth was off and interviewing. The Landseths loved cameras, and the house was loaded with color photographs of their latest expeditions. For a year or so they went on a video kick, but the cameras were too bulky and they gave it up. Heidi was relieved. She could pretend to admire a pack of photos for ten seconds, but a video required seating, and snacks, and lights off, and commentary. There was a limit to Heidi's interest.

There was one problem with such happy parents, however.

What kept them happy was either out of town or out of the country.

There had always been a housekeeper, a grounds keeper, and a nanny for Heidi, but her parents had never been away at the same time until she was ten. Even then, they were both careful to be home weekends. But ninth grade for them was a sky opening up like blue velvet to let in freedom. Heidi would be settled in boarding school, where parental occupation didn't matter; where both Mr. and Mrs. Landseth could be away months at a time, and their daughter would be fine.

Heidi hated boarding school.

*Get involved!* her parents would write, phone, and demand. *Join! Be active!*

Okay, but how?

The school was competitive to get into, and competitive to survive in. Heidi did not make the tennis team; she did not get a part in the play; upperclass students filled the costume, lights, and stagehand slots. She loved to sing, but her voice was ordinary. She did not qualify for the concert choir. She got into something called "General Chorus," which was of such low musical level it never gave a concert. The school would have been embarrassed to present General Chorus to an audience.

Heidi consistently got C's. No matter how hard she tried, there was a C at the top of the paper. If she *didn't* try, there was also a C. That was even more depressing; there ought to be a difference between trying and not trying.

Heidi understood why kids rebelled. You wanted to be good at something. Hardly anybody failed to get stoned or drunk if they really tried. Hardly anybody behind the wheel of a car got a C in speeding.

But Heidi disliked anything that meant loss of control. The idea that she would behave weirdly, or loudly, or crudely, horrified her. She wanted to know what she was saying and see what she was doing. She didn't want to wake up the next day and wonder what her most recent history included.

So of course her roommates were party girls who found Heidi the most pitiful excuse for a human being they'd ever come across and spent freshman year laughing at her and excluding her.

By the end of her first year she had slowly, painfully, made precisely two friends, Karen and Jacqueline . . . both of whom transferred elsewhere the following year.

That year, her second, Heidi came home for Christmas and refused to go back. Her parents began rotating home-attendance duty.

"Will you just leave?" Heidi kept saying to them. "Mrs. Camp is here, Burke is here, I'm fine."

Burke, the grounds keeper, was very unappreciated. Basically nobody cared how he kept or didn't keep the grounds. This gave him plenty of time to indulge his hobby, which was repairing player pianos. When Heidi was little, she used to spend a lot of time at the gatehouse, watching, but you could only be interested in broken pianos so long, and then you needed to do something else.

Mrs. Camp, the housekeeper, was a single parent who had raised three kids of her own at Dove House. They were much older than Heidi, and she hardly knew them. Mrs. Camp's rooms were on the second floor of the wing connecting Dove House to the garages and stable.

Burke and Mrs. Camp made all decisions regarding Dove House, from plumbing repairs to grocery shopping, which was the way everybody liked it. "We'll earn the money," Heidi's mother would say, "you spend it." Burke and Mrs. Camp thought this was a fine arrangement.

Burke had National Guard this weekend and was off somewhere cleaning tanks and priming guns, or whatever Weekend Warriors did.

Mrs. Camp had the flu, Heidi had taken her a bowl of soup, but Mrs. Camp moaned, "Don't come in, you'll catch this from me. I'll be okay in twenty-four hours, Honeybunch."

Mrs. Camp had called her Honeybunch since birth. Burke called her Horse, which Heidi hoped referred to her former hobby and not her looks. Her father called her Heidi Lynn, and her mother said Heidi-eidi-O.

At boarding school, nobody had called her anything.

But if she had expected things to be better in town, she was mistaken. The regional public high school was large, and she knew nobody because she had gone to Country Day through eighth grade. She seemed unable to introduce herself or to break in. The class had an impermeable membrane around it; she felt as fragile as a soap bubble lying on its exterior.

Heidi had become curiously resigned to her exile. She even thought of it that way: she was in another country and would someday go home.

# Two

*Saturday: 5:15 P.M.*

Kissing their mother good-bye made them feel guilty, so they hadn't.

Daniel, the older, was fifteen and still so consumed by anger it was difficult for him to face either parent. His mother should have behaved differently, that was all, and kept the marriage together. Daniel could not forgive Mom for allowing Dad to divorce her. As for Dad, he should not have played around with Linda. Dad certainly shouldn't be marrying the woman. Daniel could not imagine calling Linda "Mother." He couldn't imagine calling her anything except four-letter words, all of which he had practiced on Linda in the past.

But this was a wedding. You couldn't say things like that at weddings. And Linda's family would be there; she had a huge family. Dad made them sound like the best family in the world, ignoring the fact that up until two years ago, Dad, Daniel, Tuck, and Mom had been the best family in the world. Daniel was going to have to be polite at this wedding, an unimaginable thing, but he had promised both his grandmothers.

Politeness rots, thought Daniel.

Daniel was rather hoping for a high set of stone stairs down which to throw Linda just prior to the wedding vows.

He looked out the plane window. His brother, of course, had the window seat. If there was anything to see, Daniel could not see it. A whole country slipping by beneath him, and he didn't even have a window seat.

His brother, Tucker, was barely thirteen. Tuck was no use to anybody at any time and worse now. Tuck had no skills at all, no visible personality, no nothing going for him. Daniel didn't even like Tuck.

He used to like Tuck. Two years ago, when they were a family. Tuck had been a person. Now he was thirteen; divorce had made Tuck worse than bat urine. Daniel supposed some things could not be blamed on the divorce, such as war and inflation, but other than that, Daniel held his mother, father, and this Linda creep one hundred percent responsible.

"Maybe you're failing English because you didn't read the assignments," his father said a few weeks ago on the phone.

"No," said Daniel implacably, "it's because I'm under such stress since my family collapsed. I'm going to two counselors now, Dad." This was half true: he was going, but he wasn't talking. They were nerdballs; Daniel could not imagine telling these people how to make ice cubes, let alone exposing his heart to them.

His father heaved a huge sigh. Daniel loved that sigh. He figured enough of those sighs and his father would come home.

But no; his father was marrying Linda.

Linda would probably wear some floor-length white gown and have ten bridesmaids dressed in vegetable yellow, and a church full of smelly flowers, and all these relatives who would coo at the sight of Dad's handsome sons. Daniel wished he were six, because a six-year-old could puke on demand, ruin everybody's clothes, and get away with it, but a fifteen-year-old had to be pleasant.

Pleasant. What a disgusting thought.

It was enough to make him hope the plane crashed. That would delay the old wedding a few hours.

Or better yet, somebody should die. Dad wouldn't get married if his son had to be buried because of going to Dad's wedding. That would ruin Dad's life pretty well.

Daniel decided it would be better for Tuck to die than him, because Tuck was virtually dead anyway, with that personality.


*Saturday: 5:17 P.M.*


Teddie sat very still. This was only her second plane flight. She was not worried about the plane staying in the air, but she was worried that when it came down, Mommy and Daddy might not be at the airport to meet her. Gramma and Poppy had insisted that Mommy and Daddy would be there. "But what if they're not?" Teddie asked.

"Then you stay with the airline hostess until they come."

"But what if that's a year?"

"It won't be a year, Teddie. Ten minutes if they can't find a parking space."

"But what if they never find a parking space?"

"Then Daddy will keep driving in circles while Mommy runs in to get you."

"But what if Mommy gets hit by a car and nobody every comes for me?"

"That won't happen," said Gramma. "Now, stop worrying, Teddie. You're a big girl. Big girls fly by themselves across the country all the time. You just look out the window and have a good trip."

"But what if I get hungry?"

"Then the flight attendant will bring you a snack."

"But what if she can't tell I'm hungry?"

"Then you flag her down and ask her to bring you something."

"But I don't have a flag."

Poppy said she could use her hand. Teddie didn't want to stick her hand out in the aisle. She wanted it safely in her lap, around Bear. Bear was exceptionally soft; his stuffing could squash down into almost nothing if you really wanted to cram him into a small space, and if you didn't, Bear would burst out in cuddly white softness and fill up your arms.

"What if I have to make a phone call?" said Teddie.

"We put a card in your pocket, honey, you know that. It has our phone number and Mommy and Daddy's phone number."

"But what if I don't have money for the phone?"

"Then you ask the flight attendant to help you."

"But what if she's busy?"

"You don't need money, anyway," said Poppy. "That bottom number on the card, that's the credit card number; you tell the telephone operator that number."

"It's too big," said Teddie. "What if I get the numbers wrong?"

Gramma and Poppy came up with a quarter, which they taped to Teddie's palm with two Mickey Mouse Band-Aids. The quarter was warm now, and she could feel its roundness against her palm. If she had to make a phone call she could do it without using all those numbers. Teddie was not fond of numbers. She wasn't fond of letters, either.

She had expected she would learn to read the first day of kindergarten, and she was depressed that she had been in kindergarten forever and ever and ever, and still she could not read. It seemed so unfair that in order to read books like grown-ups, you had to know all those letters.

Everybody else on the plane had read a plastic card in the pocket attached to the seat in front. Teddie pulled hers out and studied the pictures. There were ways to get out of the airplane by sliding down little chutes. Teddie frowned at the pictures. It looked as if she would have to let go of Bear to do that. Teddie resolved to take the regular way out. She wasn't doing anything if she couldn't do it with Bear.

*Saturday: 5:20* P.M.

Darienne hated waiting.

She had had to wait in line to check her luggage and wait in line to board the plane, and now she had to wait in the aisle of the plane while old ladies wondered dimly where seat 37B was ("Right there," said Darienne sharply) and over-weight middle-aged men stopped to wriggle out of too-small overcoats before sitting down.

When, finally, she had gotten into her seat, she was next to some little girl clutching a teddy bear. Darienne could not believe it, but the girl's name was Teddie and the bear's name was Bear.

A family strong in imagination, Darienne thought. Probably have a dog named Dog.

Darienne had gotten the last available magazine, which turned out to be *Sports Illustrated.* Darienne despised sports. Anything involving sweat made her ill. Across the aisle from her, an obese woman in a poorly fitting corduroy suit that looked as if she had gotten it at a garage sale had *Glamour.* "Will you please switch magazines with me?" asked Darienne, taking the edge of the woman's *Glamour.*

"I haven't even opened it yet," the woman said. (As if reading *Glamour* was going to help her any.)

Then the woman left her magazine unopened on her lap, just to be obnoxious.

The plane, of course, had been late taking off.

Darienne wanted to scream.

She had a connection to make, and there was only an hour and ten minutes between flights. If they screwed up, and she missed her flight to London, she would commit several homicides. She hated people who did not have their act together.

"Why is the plane late?" she asked the flight attendant. The woman was old; she should have retired twenty years ago. *Betsey!* said her name plate.

"We're stacked up," *Betsey!* said, smiling widely as if being stacked up made *Betsey!* happy. "I'm very sorry, but there's nothing we can do."

Darienne pointed out the necessity of taking off on time, explaining that she was going to London for the week, but the hostess concentrated on giving the little Teddie creep a special Flight Pin, and a special Flight Fun Kit, and a special Before Take Off Snack.

Teddie, thought Darienne. One of those unisex, all-purpose names for when you can't tell if it's a boy or a girl. An It.

Teddie was such a dweeb, it actually enjoyed breaking through the plastic wrap to find out what colors the four enclosed crayons were. "Oh, red!" it exclaimed, as if red were the whole reason for being on the plane to start with. "Would you color with me?" it asked Darienne.

I can't stand this, Darienne thought. "Miss!" she called sharply.

The flight attendant ignored her.

Darienne grabbed the woman's little military jacket and jerked on it. "Miss, I want to switch seats."

*Betsey!* said the plane was full.

"I don't like children," Darienne said.

Teddie wrapped its geeky arms around its geeky stuffed animal, a squishy thing of the sort that crowded second-rate gift shops.

*Betsey!* said she was sure that in the course of the flight, the two of them would become friends. She said maybe Darienne could show Teddie how to trace her hand with the crayon and make a pretty picture for Teddie to give Mommy and Daddy when they met Teddie at the airport. *Betsey!* beamed at Teddie, glared at Darienne, and moved on.

A baby several rows behind Darienne began whining: revving its little lung motors and changing gears into a high-pitched shriek. Darienne closed her eyes. Was the whole flight going to be like this? What had happened to the olden days, when only civilized people could afford to fly? Why couldn't people with screaming babies take the bus?

Darienne pulled out a paperback she had just bought in the airport book shop, the newest by her favorite author: a fat book she could trust to be packed with sex, scandal, and slime. Four pages along, she realized this was not the newest title; it was the oldest, reissued;

she had read this stupid book years before. They had ripped her off, putting it on the shelf as if it were new.

*I'm stuck on a late plane next to a wimpy little kid. I'm surrounded by fat old people who won't share their magazines, babies that scream, rude hostesses, and I've already read the book I brought on board.*

Darienne baked in her own hostility. The plane was an oven, cooking her; she was a custard, she would set, and become solid resentment.

*Saturday: 5:25 P.M.*

Carly hung onto the armrests as the plane took off, lifting safely into the sky. When the plane lurched, she knew they were going to crash. Prayer expanded in her brain like an egg broken in a skillet, and then the plane evened out.

Nothing was wrong.

Nobody else so much as twitched.

She gave a silly little giggle, and her seat partner, a pleasant-looking business man older than her parents, smiled understandingly without actually looking at her. He had a laptop computer on which he was busily working. Carly thought it was pretty clever that he could be friendly without using syllables or eye contact.

*It would be nice,* thought Carly, *if there were an incredibly hand-some young man on this plane. The boy would develop a crush on her and be so in love that by the end of the flight he would come home with her, stay with her forever, meet her family, woo her.* She loved that word "woo." So nineteenth century. So courteous.

Carly studied the passengers. Babies, kids, families, business people, and a few of those weirdos you saw only when traveling: people with impossible clothes, crazy eyes, or peculiarly shaped bodies.

No cute guys.

What else was new?

The plane tilted. She had a momentary view of dwindling parking lots and housetops, and then there was only sky, which was blue and thin.

Carly had the obligatory worries about plane crashes. She considered the odds (one in two million; she'd looked it up).

Plane-crash worry was unique. You couldn't do anything. It wasn't like the past, about which Carly had said to herself a million times, If I'd done this, if I'd said this, if I'd been a better person, if, if, if . . .

No, if the plane crashed, it was Their Fault. Carly didn't have to say, Listen, I'm sorry, I know I should have done ten hundred things differently.

Carly much preferred problems that were somebody else's fault. That way she could shake her head and sigh, the way she did for acid rain and inner-city warfare, but she didn't actually have to see where she'd gone wrong and wonder if she'd ever go right again.

*I'm going home*, Carly's heart sang, very country and western, with twangs and tunes, *I'm going home, to say I'm sorry*.

You haven't said you're sorry yet, she reminded herself. They might not care how sorry you are. They might not even meet the plane.

She shivered slightly. She imagined the airport. Would Shirl be there? Would Mom and Dad? Would they hold out their arms? When she said *I'm sorry*, would they whisper, *It doesn't matter, we love you?*

Or would she stand in the terminal, surrounded by chairs bolted to the floor, while travelers broke around her like tide over a sandbar, and be alone? Would she have to take a bus to the house? What if they didn't let her in? What if—

I have only one thing to offer, thought Carly. I really am sorry. I have to believe that that matters to them.

Actually, she did have something else to offer.

She had knit her twin a sweater: cable stitches; quite complex. It looked pretty darn good. Carly had enjoyed knitting it. Of course she had started the sweater for herself, just as she had started everything for herself last year; last year Carly had not cared about a single person on earth except herself. She had chosen a heathery wool—rich, rusty purple. She and her twin were fair and looked ill in pastels but fragile and beautiful in dark, intense colors. Shirl would love the color, but Shirl might still be so mad that she'd never wear it, or would trash it, or give it away.

Not much of a peace offering. Considering what Carly had done.

Carly had not packed the sweater in her luggage but wrapped it in sparkly tissue and tucked it into a clear plastic bag. It lay under the seat in front. She smiled down at the shiny package.

The timelessness of flight droned around her; the rituals of ordering a soda, putting down the little white tray on which to set her soda, watching the safety demonstration video, scanning the flight magazine in the pouch—all this was correct. It was right and just that she should have these few hours aloft; literally above her problems and the people she had to face.

She was amazed at her contentment. The year of vicious rebellion seemed as distant as the miles they covered.

When the flight attendant brought the meal, Carly beamed at her. *Betsey!* said the name tag. Carly loved that exclamation point. *Betsey!* looked like the kind of woman who turned everything into an exclamation point. I'd like to be like that, thought Carly. Maybe I could do this when I grow up.

Carly laughed at herself. She was a little behind on the growing-up scale. A little behind on the educational scale, too.

But I'll catch up, thought Carly. She liked the way *Betsey!* had cut her hair, too: a thick, buoyant cut that looked somehow fluffy and long and yet was really quite short and easy to care for. Carly touched her own shoulder-length hair and thought, Yes. I'm going to cut it. Layers. I'm going to look suburban again, and flight attendant-ish, and have it all together.

How pretty the tray was, with its little dessert sparkling cinnamon on top, its carrots bright orange, and its gravy rich brown. "Lovely," Carly told *Betsey!* although usually she did not care for airline food.

Carly laughed at herself and then tucked her smile back in, to be a rational, sober copy of the rest of the passengers.

What more beautiful words exist, thought Carly Foyle, than *going home?*

# Three

*Saturday:* 5:30 P.M.

Laura and Ty had been in the last EMT training class. All one hundred and ninety hours of training had been fascinating. All necessary. Failure to pass the state test was rare, not because the test was simple, but because if you were motivated to start and to stay, you were motivated to learn the techniques and get them right.

Mr. Farquhar was the chief instructor. He was patient and funny and always made you feel special for making the effort at all. "Remember, kids," he would say, "we've got a town full of rich people, estate people, summer people, and they expect to be rescued. They never expect to do the rescuing. We don't get volunteers from that quarter."

There were certainly no rich people in the training sessions, nor had Laura come across any on the crew. It was as blue collar as changing tires or bagging groceries.

She had wondered why. A lot of the wealthy townspeople were very community oriented; always serving on this board or that, sponsoring this fund-raiser or that. Mr. Farquhar summed it up with a shrug of his eyebrows. "They don't like to get their hands dirty," he said, "and this is a dirty job. People vomit on you and bleed on you. Their houses or their bodies smell bad. You'll step in car oil and broken glass."

Laura had fallen mildly in love with Patrick, who assisted his father in the instruction. Everybody had to take turns being victim and being rescuer. Laura wanted to be Patrick's victim, but of course somebody else got Patrick. Laura ended up, time after time, with Ty Maronn.

Just because you both wanted to be ambulance volunteers didn't mean you had anything else in common.

Laura and Ty couldn't abide each other.

Laura said Ty had no personality. "He's sort of like an undershirt," she would say. "You could fold him up, or stuff him in a corner, or wear him inside out, and you'd never notice one way or the other."

Ty felt Laura had far too much personality. "She can't stand anything unless it's her show," he said to any other trainee who would listen. "She has to be in charge. If she's not in charge, she certainly wants to be the one most seriously hurt, getting the most attention."

Saturday afternoon was sluggish and gray.

Winter had lasted too long; everybody was sick of it; everybody wanted to be in Florida or the Bahamas. But what with school, and lack of money, all they could do was party.

Laura and Ty were at the same party. This particular party had started too early. It had no purpose and no plan: just a bunch of people in the same living room, drinking sodas right now but getting bored, looking around for more; ready for beer, for cruel gossip instead of chatter, for sex instead of laughter.

It was not a particularly nice party.

Nice people, Laura thought, I like all these people. But any minute now the party's going to go bad.

She was not sure what to do about it. She'd come with a girlfriend and therefore didn't have her own car. The girlfriend had vanished, and it was not the kind of party where Laura felt comfortable poking in dark rooms looking for somebody.

Laura was on call Monday. It being Saturday, she did not have her scanner with her. She was not thinking of rescues or fires. She was thinking drearily of the paper she and her parents had signed about them coming to get her if there was drinking and drugs, no questions asked. She was thinking—But nothing is happening. I can't call them when nothing is happening.

Which, perversely, made Laura feel like starting something. Everybody in the room was ready to start something. The group was working itself up, teetering on the edge. The decision was in the air— whether to join in and even goad the others along when trouble started or whether to deflect it.


*Saturday: 5:35 P.M.*


Heidi was waist-deep in dogs. She was not in a dog mood. Her mother had ankle biters; miniatures with wrinkled bodies like stacked pancakes. Heidi could hardly tolerate Winnie and Clemmie. She didn't even consider them dogs, just little yippy things she wished would run away and forage in the woods. Her father's dog was a long, lean, award-winning Irish setter who required brushing, grooming, de-ticking, walking, and love. Fang could not go ten minutes without whining for more attention. (Heidi knew how that felt, but tried to keep herself from actually whimpering out loud.)

"Come, here, Fang." she said resignedly, and the dog, tail brutally whacking furniture, climbed all over her.

Heidi was sturdier than she wanted to be.

Fashion these days required you to be anorexic. Her short friends were size three, and her tall friends were size eight. Naked or clothed, you couldn't tell they needed bras. Their clothes fit perfectly. Heidi was dramatically curved. She had read that men liked this, but you couldn't prove it by Heidi. All she knew was that her clothes did not fit perfectly.

Everybody else took aerobics and jazzercise. They hopped and danced and flung and arched. "I'd need a shelf under my bosom to do that," Heidi said, and the gym instructor, whose shape was basically inverted, said, "Nonsense, Heidi."

Heidi never wore makeup. She had naturally red cheeks, long lashes, and bright lips. Her eyes were plain brown, her hair even plainer.

Mrs. Camp's dog was an elderly mutt named Tally-Ho. Tally-Ho was a great dog; a tan four-legged thing with a great personality. Like me, thought Heidi. If you'd get to know me, I have a wonderful personality. Otherwise I'm just this brown-haired, two-legged thing.

Fang was handsome (his real name was Dove House Prince Albert) and also stupid. Once let outdoors, Fang would go insane and try to explore all Litchfield County in one afternoon. So Fang always had to be on a leash.

Tally, however, was a sensible guy who sniffed only at scents close at hand and never got sufficiently excited to follow them. Tally hated to let Mrs. Camp out of his sight, but when Mrs. Camp's doors were shut, Tally would accept Heidi.

If Burke calls me Horse and Mrs. Camp called me Honeybunch, thought Heidi, Tally probably calls me Second Best.


*Saturday: 5:37 P.M.*

The airport lounge was done in two colors: light gray and dark gray. Chairs were bolted to the floor as if passengers on their way to

Dallas or Tokyo might otherwise take one along. The chairs were collected in groups of six. Chrome arms prevented children from lying on their parents' laps or exhausted travelers from snoozing in a prone position. Cylinders of driveway gravel stood at the end of each row, ready to accept cigarette butts and trash.

A small, thin man in a dark red, ill-fitting suit continuously plied the floors with a dustpan on wheels and a long-handled broom.

Two men and two women in airline uniforms continually talked on their telephones, their voices nicely modulated.

Many people never sat but circulated among the chairs and video screens. Some read newspapers, some magazines; some stared blankly into space.

Waiting induces coma.

Time expands.

Minutes are years.

The soft gray carpeting ran right up the walls, so that the crowds of people waiting to meet arriving planes were wrapped on all sides in carpet, like presents in a gift box.

Few talked. They seemed to have finished their talk in the car, driving to the airport, or to be reserving their talk for when the passengers landed.

They were suspended until the plane chose to arrive, until weather cooperated, until luggage was delivered. Then their personalities and chatter could reemerge. They would rise up like otters breaking through the cool surface of a pond.

Teddie's father considered his filming strategy. He loved filming his daughter. They had had their only child late in life, when the excitement of careers and travel and furnishing a fine home had palled, and Teddie was the most important thing that had ever happened to them. It was impossible to image why they had waited so long to have a child. And this child! Having Teddie was like winning the lottery: she was sweet, beautiful, funny, and smart.

Every evening, Teddie's father could hardly wait to come home from work. Even though she was five now, Teddie still charged through the house, flung herself down the stairs, and hurled herself onto his body, shrieking, "Daddy!" in a voice of total joy.

She would not run like that here at the airport. In public Teddie insisted on being "grown-up." Besides, she would probably come out holding the stewardess's hand. But if Teddie did let go of the escorting hand and race toward him, which would he rather have: the first hug in two weeks or a really good film of her running forward?

She might run to hug her mother first, although Teddie's relationship with her mother was much calmer; they were more apt to kiss than to smother. In that case, he could get a really great shot of Affection at the Airport. He laughed to himself. Years ago, he'd have been embarrassed by his own adoration of his own kid; now he reveled in it; couldn't wait to do it again. He loved designing video programs of Teddie: her name on the screen, a title for the activity. He had a whole library of Teddie.

Teddie's father glanced upward at the screen that listed all planes landing; Teddie's was still ON TIME. The plane wasn't even due for nearly forty minutes. His wife, as worried as Teddie was about hitting traffic, or getting a flat tire, or finding a parking space, had made him leave home far too early.

He shifted the burden of the camcorder. He smiled at his wife. She had bought a magazine especially to read at the airport, but she was simply turning pages. She was afraid of planes. He knew her stomach was in knots, worrying. He patted her hand, and she smiled at him, the taut, nervous smile of a mother whose child is not yet home.


*Saturday: 5:38 P.M.*


It was a curiously ugly night.

Snow left from the last storm made a grim patchwork on the hillside below Dove House. The rolling lawn seemed filled by black holes ready to suck up unwary trespassers. The trees clanked when they swayed. The ice on each twig sounded more like stainless steel than tinkling bells. The rose garden, breathtaking in bloom, was nothing more than bare ground with sharp, jabbing stems.

The moon was not a graceful orb but a mis-shapen circle. No stars were visible. It spooked Heidi that the moon was so clear and the stars so missing. Even as she looked out, the sky around the moon darkened threateningly. It did not seem cold enough for snow. They would have one of those grim, depressing, icy rains that seemed to be a Dove House winter specialty.

Heidi had once read an article on weather (one reading surely was enough for the subject) and learned that out West, say Minnesota, once it got cold, it stayed cold. You didn't have thaws, variety, and unknowns in your winter temperature. The Northeast should be so lucky. Snow never stayed on the ground because within a day or two it was bound to warm up and melt off. Snow could fall ten miles north of Heidi and be rain at Dove House.

Heidi always started thinking of supper when the sky darkened, even though supper was hours away. She did a thorough inspection of refrigerator, pantry, and freezer, food being a top priority for Heidi. Her boarding school friends Karen and Jacqueline had hardly ever eaten anything. Heidi adored calories.

Perhaps with Mrs. Camp asleep at the far end of the house and her parents away, she would have Chocolate Dinner. Chocolate sauce on ice cream for a main course, chocolate pudding with whipped cream for a vegetable, chocolate cookies and chocolate cake with chocolate icing and chocolate jimmies for dessert.

I'd have to call the ambulance, she thought. Bet they've never had a Chocolate Overdose call before.

The dogs whined.

She didn't mind Fang and Tally-Ho whining; they were adult about it, just mentioning that they needed to go outside. Winnie and Clemmie, however, moaned and sobbed. Worthless excuses for dogs. When Fang, Winnie, and Clemmie finished up, Heidi stuck them back in the house while she and Tally went out into the early evening.

The temperature was dropping and the moon glared.

The wind came in gusts, separate ribbons that attacked her legs, then ripped through her hair. It seemed to blow all ways at once, as if fighting itself.

Tally stayed close, as if *she* had to protect *him*.


*Saturday:* 5:39 P.M.


Daniel and Tuck's father had not brought Linda. He'd wanted to. It would help his sons realize that now another family was starting up, with Linda the new fourth member.

But Linda said that was ridiculous; Daniel and Tuck did not want a new fourth member; Daniel and Tuck were hoping for a slick spot on the road that would send Linda into bloody orbit.

"Now, now," said Mr. MacArthur. "The boys are very civilized."

Linda looked at her future husband. "There is no such thing," said Linda, "as a civilized boy. That's what a boy is—something *un*civilized."

So Tuck and Daniel's father was at the airport alone.

He was working out a strategy.

If Daniel decided to be rotten, the boy could be seriously, strongly rotten. Rotten was definitely one of Daniel's subspecialties.

So in what order should they do things to sort of taper off Daniel's rage? Should they first go into the airport restaurant for ice cream? Sit there in neutral territory and talk about nothing much until they were relaxed with each other? Or should they do the little airport chores—get luggage, retrieve car, etc? That would give them something to talk about: where is the luggage, where is the short-term parking exit? And then drive for half an hour, find a McDonald's, and then relax?

Of course, he had no idea what they were going to talk about once they were relaxed. ("Well, the wedding plans are in great shape, boys." "Don't worry, Dad, we'll ruin them.")

His ex-wife had called to say the boys' plane had taken off safely. She was courteous and correct. They should appoint her ambassador to someplace tricky. He had said, "Thank you, June. I'm setting off for the airport now."

"The boys promised to be pleasant."

This was difficult to believe. But he said. "That's wonderful, June. It's very nice of you to encourage the boys to have a good attitude."

"I did not encourage them to have a good attitude," said his ex-wife, in a voice like a razor blade. "I encouraged them to swear less."

He took a deep breath. "Do you want me to call when they've landed?"

"Daniel will call," she said.

"Great. That's settled, then. Great." He was sweating buckets.

But now, at the airport, he was not thinking of his ex-wife or his future wife. He was thinking of his sons: they would be teenagers three thousand miles away, without him, and that was his choice. He would see them only a few weeks and a few weekends for the rest of their childhood, and that was his choice. He had put Linda ahead of them. They knew it.

How much had they grown since he'd seen them last? What were the newest words in their extensive swear vocabulary?

Tuck had been sweet and gentle in elementary school, but he emerged into seventh grade like a stock car going into the final lap: roaring, screaming, leaving patches.

As for Daniel, Daniel had been difficult every day of his life; there was no argument he could not offer ten times more than his parents could stand to hear. There was no weekend when Daniel could not ruin the nicest outing. There was no bedtime when Daniel could not spring the worst possible news on his parents, to keep them from sleeping well yet again.

And yet Daniel captivated his father. Daniel seemed to him to be a man trapped in a kid's body; a huge balloon of a personality caught in the confines of schoolrooms. A laughing delight imprisoned by homework and sports.

Someday Daniel would emerge and be the shining star of his father's world.

Unless he hates me, thought Mr. MacArthur.

He thought that they should get the luggage first, find the car, and then stop for a hamburger, when the abrasive edge of actually meeting was worn down a little.


*Saturday: 5:40 P.M.*


Shirl had not driven into the airport; urban traffic was far too terrifying for a seventeen-year-old. She had taken the limousine, which was actually a large bus, and she and Carly would take it back again to the suburbs. Shirl navigated the immense airport, stumbling around, trying to locate the gate where her twin's flight would come in. She found it at last. She walked through it, making herself comfortable with its outlines, identifying the door out of which her sister would come. Then she walked back a few hundred yards down the airport leg and got herself a ginger ale. The little bubbles tickled her throat.

I'm not mad anymore, thought Shirl.

It was like being set free from prison.

For a whole year, rage had percolated through Shirl like an endless pot of coffee. Sometimes she could feel the acid of fury right in her veins. She was taking chemistry and she thought if they analyzed her blood, the samples would be different from anybody else's. Pure rage would burst her blood cells, pack her arteries.

Whenever she had thought of Carly—and how could you not think of your own twin all the time?—she would get hot and violent inside her skin.

But then came Thanksgiving.

Carly did not communicate.

Then came Christmas.

Carly did not so much as send a postcard.

How terrifying it was to have holidays without love.

Holidays without family.

Mom and Dad and Shirl struggled to Give Thanks and to be Christmassy without Carly, but it had not worked. To celebrate, you needed to be whole. You did not have to have everybody there in person, but in spirit, oh, yes! They all had to be present in their hearts.

At first Shirl held Carly wholly responsible, but as January passed and cold, bleak, ugly February began, Shirl lost interest in who deserved blame. Who even cared?

Let's just be a family again, Shirl thought.

They were twins, but they had not followed even slightly the same path. While Shirl got good grades and volunteered at the hospital and was tremendously proud of her position on the first-ever volleyball team at the high school, Carly got into parties.

Parties where kids trashed houses, stole money, and did drugs.

Parties where the police were called.

Parties where nobody, Carly especially, seemed to be having fun; they were having violence.

Carly quit high school, stopped living at home, stole money from her own family, and finally, with some of her scary sick friends, headed for California.

*At sixteen.*

Shirl at sixteen did not feel equipped to make breakfast yet.

Here was Shirl, an ordinary suburban kid who loved her family and her friends and her little school-ish routines—and here was her twin, living on the street somewhere across the world. Here was Shirl, yearning for different posters on her walls, hoping for lacier sheets for her bed, and there was her twin, homeless by choice.

And then came the letter.

The first words from Carly in ten months.

The letter was a love song—to California and her family. The letter said, "I went to a counseling service they have here for runaways.

Everybody has been so nice to me. Nobody has been mad at me. Californians are like their weather; sunshine every day, no matter how stormy I am. I want to come home. They say it's time for me to go back home, and they are right. Will you take me back? I want to start over. Please don't be mad. Love, Carly."

The letter.

Shirl's mother wept. Her father, trying not to get his hopes up, having been slapped so often and so hard by Carly, said cynically, "She just needs money."

The letter. Her grandparents read a thousand messages into it. They were all for going to California, hugging those wonderful sunshine people, getting Carly themselves.

Shirl put her foot down. "She's my twin," said Shirl, "and I'm the one who is going to meet her at the airport."

"We're all going," said her parents and grandparents.

"No. I'm bringing her home. I want to do that. We're twins. I have to be the one."

Her mother, who had not cooked in years, cooked up a storm. Her grandmother, who had never cooked to start with, stocked up on food as if Carly's only hope was eating. Her father suddenly painted Carly's bedroom walls. The room still smelled paint-ish. The letter sat in the center of the dining table, to be held, fingered, folded, reread whenever anybody passed through the room.

*Carly's coming home. We'll be a family again.*

Shirl won the argument. There was something mystic about being twins, even failed twins like Carly and Shirl. Her parents finally said Yes, she could go alone. Her grandparents finally said Yes, we'll wait here.

Shirl went by herself. But she would not be coming home by herself. She would have her twin to hold, she would be a twin again. She would say to her sister, whom she loved, *I'm sorry, too.*

Shirl was one of the ones who could not sit but stood a few feet away from the TV monitor, sipping her soda, studying the line that meant Carly: Flight One One Six. She was breathless, and excited, and very very close to tears. *My sister. My sister is coming home.*

# Four

Tuck was fast asleep, drooped over the seat, his neck almost severed by the hard plastic cover on his magazine, which had stayed in reading position even when he fell asleep on top of it. Daniel was sort of awake, awake enough to hear the flight attendant say sharply that they were to fasten seat belts. He had his on, but Tuck's was off.

The plane changed angles abruptly. We're here already! thought Daniel, and he was afraid. Afraid of meeting his father and Linda; afraid of a new family; afraid of his own temper. What if his fury exploded during the ceremony—"Don't you do this! I hate you!"—when everybody else was laughing and happy? Then they would hate Daniel, all these new people that so frightened and outraged him.

Daniel's stomach lifted up to fill his throat. He could not believe how swiftly they were landing. He reached for Tuck's seat belt to pull it over Tuck's lap and buckle it, but the plastic magazine cover was in the way. It was *Popular Science*, and the cover looked interesting. Daniel was sorry he had not noticed it before.

Behind Daniel somebody screamed, a horrible high-pitched scream that he heard not in his ears but in his spine, so that he curled forward in the seat. Daniel's fingers closed around Tuck's seat-belt latch.

The flight attendant's voice was fierce; it was full of force, like his mother's when she kicked Dad out. "Clasp your hands on top of your head!" shouted the flight attendant, her voice turned up like a boom box. "Bend over! *Stay down!*"

"God!" screamed somebody in the back. "We're crashing!"

*Saturday: 5:41:12* P.M.

Darienne checked her watch. It was a lovely watch, one in her extensive collection of watches; a circle of jadelike stone with four tiny diamonds to mark 12, 3, 6, and 9. She admired her wrist, which was slim, and her hands, which were exquisite. She admired her blouse, which had tight sleeves blurry with watercolored leaves and spinning falling flowers. The neck was high, with two bands of dark red, and the general effect was of a girl from Victorian times, a girl of wealth and leisure, of beauty and grace.

It did not entirely satisfy Darienne to look down, so she reached into her leather handbag and took out a small mirror. She admired her features. Really, at school it was considered correct to complain about how you looked. Darienne thought that was ridiculous and never went along with it. She looked wonderful all the time and she knew it.

Across the aisle the plump woman who had refused to exchange *Glamour* with her said, "Please help me. I can't seem to fasten my seat belt." There was a note of frenzy in her voice, which surprised Darienne. The flight attendant had been babbling at the front of their section, but Darienne made it a point never to listen to stewardesses. It was repetitive, all that blather about oxygen masks, and how to give them to babies (after yourself, which Darienne thought reasonable). Besides, what was a stewardess except a glorified waitress? You were supposed to call them "flight attendants" now. Darienne didn't mind, as long as it was Darienne they attended. But *Betsey!* had failed to do that. *Betsey!* had been solely interested in the little dweeb Teddie.

Darienne looked curiously at the matronly passenger to see what caused such distress.

The woman's mouth had opened as if she were yawning deeply, but a scream was emerging: an immense, shattering scream, the likes of which Darienne had never heard before: a scream such as primitive soldiers must have given as they rode into battle with lances pointed. The woman's lipstick was fresh; she had just reapplied it. The scream was framed in an orange shade that Darienne found particularly repellent.

The woman's seat belt dangled in the aisle. The woman's hands scrabbled in the wrong place.

The plane jolted. It seemed to be a child's toy now, which somebody was taking apart to reassemble for another project. Darienne could not believe what the plane was doing. It turned left, turned right, turned down. Planes couldn't do that. They were not jointed in the middle.

If I miss my connection, thought Darienne, I will sue.

Rain.

Heidi would have said it was too cold for rain; that the temperature was below freezing, but perhaps that was the wind chill. She and Tally-Ho walked down to the reflecting pool, to see how frozen over it was; ice came and went at this time of year; the pool was shallow, and when she was little she skated there. Skating was something you did only when you were little.

The rain was pellets now. Ice granules. Rice ice. It hurt her face, and even Tally whined.

"Okay, we'll go in," she said, thinking, I'll start a fire. Maybe she would start two fires: one in the toasty little library off the Gallery, and maybe even one in the Hall. Her mother called the big living room the Hall; it was large enough for a meeting to nominate the President. Heidi's mother joked that if they ever ran out of money, they could host conventions in the Hall. The Hall had a stone fireplace two stories high, rustic and yet imposing. A fire in the Hall fireplace didn't take mere split logs, but trees. Starting a fire in the Hall was a major undertaking.

But what else did she have to do on a Saturday night?

Pathetic, thought Heidi. Sixteen years old and all you can think of to do is melt chocolate and light a fire.

The noise began.

Noise like an electric guitar stuck on one note, while the acoustics engineer turned the volume up, and up, and up, and up. A thrumming single note that sucked in the world.

The noise expanded like a planet exploding.

Like war.

A wind with the force of a fire truck's hose lifted her hair right out of the hood of her tied-tight jacket. One of her mittens was actually sucked off her hand. Her scream she could feel in her throat but not hear; she was deaf; the entire world was screaming.

It was huge and black. A flying saucer, a nuclear bomb, a tornado on its side.

It was in her yard, in her rose garden.

Heidi's scream threw her to her knees.

*Saturday: 5:41:20 P.M.*

Carly had taken off her seat belt to reach beneath the seat ahead of her and hold the sweater, as if she could hold her twin, her childhood, good times, love.

And then weirdly, she who had little flight experience, she who had no grounds for comparison, knew that whatever maneuver the plane was doing was abnormal. The force, the sound, the angle—it was all wrong.

The flight attendant suddenly interrupted, saying in a harsh, almost scalding voice, "Everybody fasten seat belts. *Fasten seat belts*. Clasp your hands on top of your head! Bend over as far as you can!"

Carly was momentarily diverted by the prettiness of *Betsey!*'s uniform: the wine red silk bow tied beneath the white collar, perfectly offsetting the dark gray militarylike jacket. Nice outfit, thought Carly. I'd like to do this, too. I'd be good at this.

In the nanosecond before she accepted what was happening, Carly watched a thousand thoughts race through the flight attendant's mind and be discarded; everything condensed. "Bend over!" the woman shouted. "Stay down!"

The plane inverted.

*Saturday: 5:41:30 P.M.*

Heidi struggled to figure out the origin of the sound, but like the wind, it came all ways at once, attacking her. A noise so great it entered her spine, penetrated her brain cells, would kill her by volume alone.

Her eyes filled with the water of horror, as she crouched, trying to escape its notice, while her mind screamed, *Dear God! Dear God!* and she was aware of how strange that was, because she was not religious and did not pray. There was time to think that she should have gotten closer to God while there was time, and time to think that maybe He would understand, and time to think *what is this?*

The black thing avoided the safe open stretch of grass and pierced the woods beyond. The tangled, twisted, spooky woods, where icy rivulets crept through ancient evergreens, over ravines littered with glacial rocks. Red lights glittered; a spray of light, as if a row of cars ahead had put on their brakes. The tops of trees were sheared off and in the dark Heidi saw darker things hurled into the air: missiles, the beginning of the ground attack.

And yet, she had already discarded that theory. Even as she was thinking of bombs and UFOs, she knew. It was a plane crash. In her woods. There were people in there. That's what those flying missiles were.

Bodies. And seats.


*Saturday: 5:41:35* P.M.


Teddie put her face directly into Bear's squishy softness. She did not mind breathing through the acrylic fur. The darkness of Bear pressed against her eyes was better than looking around. She wanted to hold hands, but she had the window on one side and the mean woman on the other. Teddie thought vaguely that windows were glass, and glass broke, and that was bad, but she did not know what to do about it and then the glass broke.


*Saturday: 5:41:36* P.M.


Daniel thought: neat. We get to use that emergency chute.

He pictured it: it was going to look sort of like a swimming-pool raft—an inflated tube or sled. He thought: I forget where the exit is, though.

He jerked the plastic magazine out from under his brother's chin, knowing that it really would decapitate Tuck, no joke. He shoved Tuck's head down toward his knees, when he realized it was not going to matter where the exit was. The plane had come apart right in front of them; the row of seats in front of Daniel's eyebrows spun away like pancakes flipped by a great spatula.

Daniel and Tuck's row, as open as an amusement park ride, hurled forward into the unforgiving branches of trees.

# Five

*Saturday: 5:42 P.M.*

Pieces of tree, pieces of metal, pieces of seat and wing gleamed in the moonlight. Some plane lights remained on, so what was left of the plane twinkled in a friendly way. The plane was immense. It seemed impossible that such a huge thing had ever been airborne. It looked bigger and longer than the house, garages, and stable. Like some incredibly large, white celestial cigar, suddenly ripped in pieces and thrown to the ground.

After the deafening roar of the engines ceased, there was a hideous grinding and gnashing of metal. Tree and rock and earth screamed as they were hit.

Then came a queer heavy silence.

She could hear the icy rain hitting the fallen plane, drumming gently on metal that should not have been there.

A single second went by, as if the world were drawing its breath.

How many human beings had that plane held? How many seats must have been crammed into that smashed cylinder? How many passengers—

Screams began. Screams for help. Screams of people's names. Primitive screams. Voices stuck on single vowels.

The ferocity with which the plane smacked the ground seemed fatal in noise alone, never mind impact. She looked at the wreckage, the stupefying array of wreckage, and could not believe there had been survivors. The plane had divided itself all over the estate, split open like samples for biopsy. It had amputated woods, flung its parts as far as the old pony field.

But people were alive in there, and they were hurt. They needed help.

For a split second, Heidi actually turned around to see who was going to help them.

I'm alone, she thought. There is nobody else to help but me. And I'm not even good enough to sing in a choir or make a friend.

Anxiety seized her chest so painfully that Heidi almost thought she, too, was wounded. *What do I do now? Where do I go? I have to do the right thing!*

She could not waste time screaming like those passengers; she was the one who had to get help. To use the telephone.

Sensible, Heidi, she said to herself, be sensible.

But she did not run toward the house with its phones and extensions; she ran toward the plane, thinking, *Pull them out—something smells—it smells like the oil delivery—what if there's a fire—get them out—*

Down the hill and far to her left, a football field away, began the noise as immense as the end of the world. Heidi whirled to see a section of plane burst into flame. One vast wing, still connected to a cut away circle of passenger seats, was on fire.

The flames stretched higher than the trees themselves. Or perhaps there were no trees; the plane had flattened that part of the woods.

The screams from the burning section were muffled. Or perhaps Heidi was deafened. She felt queerly packaged, her head and ears throbbing with white noise. She could hear another noise more clearly: panting, as if all the dogs were exhausted from running, were gasping for breath beside her.

It was her own lungs breathing like that. She had not moved since she stopped screaming herself, and she was out of breath and panting.

Impact had not killed those passengers.

But fire would.

Telephone, Heidi thought, hanging onto the word like religion. Telephone, telephone.

She ran back to the house, slipping on the horrible ice, the uphill of her yard as steep as waterslides, as impossible to scale. Her hands were both bare, she did not know what had happened to her mittens, or where Tally-Ho was. She felt as if she toiled up that hill for half an hour; they would have died before she even reached the house. She was worthless, she had failed them. She would never save a soul they would all be burned burned burned it was her fault.

The phone was weirdly difficult to recognize. She actually had to stop and think how it worked. Nine one one, she said to herself, poking her trembling finger at the little white squares on the phone.

Nobody answered.

Her facial muscles leaped in several directions, as if she were becoming a gargoyle, a monster. *"Answer me!"* Heidi screamed. She almost pounded the phone against the wall. Almost smashed it because people would not answer her.

On the fourth ring, a mild woman's voice said, "Emergency. What is your location?"

She could not believe the woman's voice was so leisurely. It made her terribly angry. "Dove House. Nearing River," said Heidi. She was shouting. She tried to control herself. Her body had the shakes. The phone was difficult to hold. "A plane crashed," she said. "In my yard. A plane crashed. In my yard." The words spurted out of her.

The voice was disembodied: so calm, so matter-of-fact, that Heidi could not imagine it being attached to flesh and blood; perhaps she was talking to a computer, or a tape. "A plane?" said the voice. "Are you sure?"

"I'm sure. It just blew up, some of it. The rest of it is in my woods."

"Where do you live?"

"An estate called Dove House, off Rockrimmon, off Old Pond Meadow." There was a pause. Heidi thought, Is this it? Do I hang up now?

The voice said, "We'll send a cruiser over to check, ma'am."

"I don't think you understand," said Heidi, her voice rising. "It's a huge plane. Like you'd take overseas. Maybe a 747 or something. There are hundreds of people down there. Some of them are alive. It's on fire! It's blowing up! It's—"

"I'm alerting Fire and Ambulance," said the voice, sounding as if the whole story were quite beyond belief. Sounding as if this were a hoax. "We'll be there as fast as we can."

Heidi thought, But then, I don't believe it, either. That's my rose garden, not my plane crash site. She whispered. "You're coming, aren't you?"

"We're coming," said the woman.

This time the voice was solid. Heidi believed. She hung up. She ran back outside.

Hours seemed to have slipped away. Precious don't-bleed-to-death hours, which she'd wasted on the phone.

She skidded down the slope to the plane section that was not on fire. People were walking around, like ghosts in the ice.

For a splintered second—all night, for Heidi, time would come in long thin divisions—she was afraid of those people.

How could they be strolling around, like tourists?

A large section of plane lay some fifty feet into the woods. She could not tell whether it was front, center, or rear. It was cut away like a diagram of a seating arrangement, and the dozen passengers exposed to view were trapped not just by the metal, but by a fir tree, an enormous spike tree that had jabbed through the plane and the people's bodies. The plane was so high. It had landed, and yet it was so high. It would take ladders to get to those people.

And on the ground, people were scattered everywhere, like confetti. Heidi stopped to assist the first one she came to: a woman sitting quietly upright. Still in her seat. How amazing. Both she and the seat had been neatly ejected. "You have to get out of here," said Heidi, quickly unfastening the seat belt. "Some of the plane is already on fire. I don't know if the rest of it will catch fire or not." She was babbling. She tried to think of the essentials: the information the woman really needed. She said, "The house is up on the hill. You—"

The woman had no shape to her. She was soggy. She was dead.

Heidi made a noise like the dogs, a keening static-y sound, and turned away.

A man walked up out of the gloom and rain. He was wearing a three-piece suit, and looked prepared to give a speech at a major convention. There seemed to be nothing wrong with him, no wounds, so he must be a neighbor, although they had no neighbors. He'd have had to walk a mile in any direction through the woods or fields to get here. The only time they had ever met any neighbors was during the Peacock Complaint era. Then she saw that he still had his seat belt on. It, and the upholstery of the seat, were still attached to him. He seemed unaware of this, and Heidi thought it would be rude to mention it. She was having great difficulty figuring out what mattered and what didn't.

He said to Heidi, "Did you telephone for help?"

"Yes. They're on the way."

"Good. Is the house open?"

"Yes," said Heidi, thinking, We can't stand here and chat. We have to do something. But what?

"I'll start moving people up to the house," he said.

He hauled a moaning woman to her feet. Putting her arm over his shoulder, he said to her, "Come on, walk, you have to, the rest of the plane is going to go, it doesn't matter how much it hurts."

*The rest of the plane is going to go,* she thought. That means the people in the fire are already gone. That means we have to get everybody here into Dove House. Now. I have to do it myself. Now.

She walked another ten feet and pulled a tree limb off the person touching her leg. "Can you walk?" she said.

"Yes," said the woman. "Go help somebody else. I can make it to the house alone."

The calm of these two passengers helped. It gave Heidi a train for her thought: Move people into the house.

Right.

Okay.

Start.

Heidi fell on a chrome pole. She staggered up. It was part of a liquor cart; tiny little bottles made a bumpy glass puddle.

She got over it, heading for the closest cry for help, but when she reached down to assist the person screaming, the person was dead. The screamer was beneath him. In the weird half-light of fire and moon and ice, the dead passenger was already a ghost. She tried to shift the body, but it was heavy and stuck to its seat. The seat itself was crushing the wounded person beneath.

"I'm coming," said Heidi stupidly. "I'm here."

She plucked and twitched, as weak as a butterfly, trying to get a handhold on the dead thing and its seat and finally came to her senses and just tipped it over. The person beneath was a little girl. A very little girl, with a leg bone sticking up into the air like a snapped broomstick.

Heidi had no idea what to do. None. She turned and screamed into the night *"Hurry up!"* Her scream blended with all the other screams, the screams for help, the screams in Spanish, the screams for Mama.

She looked at her watch. Three minutes had gone by since her phone call.

*Only three minutes.*

She was older by a decade. She was useless. She had no brain, no sense, no strength.

She did not know how to pick up a child whose bone stuck out through the flesh. "It's okay," she said idiotically to the child. "What's your name?" she added, thinking, I'm insane, this is not a tea party.

"Teddie," said the child.

Somebody crawled toward her. Heidi wanted to bolt, but instead she said, "Can you stand? I'll get you up to the house."

The person was drenched in blood. She had never seen so much blood; it was as if the person had just taken a shower. "It's mostly not mine," the person mumbled. "My leg, though. Crushed up into me."

Heidi got her arms around the person; she couldn't even tell what sex it was. "I'll be back, Teddie," she said. Like the last couple in a nightmarishly slow three-leg race, she and the bloody person hobbled up the hill until Heidi ran out of strength and just lay the person down again.

"More people are coming to help," said Heidi.

*But are they? It's been hours.*

She looked at her watch. Another minute had gone by.

*One measly minute.*

She tried to organize herself. Tried to think of a master plan here.

Twice she went back to the wreckage and twice moved a victim halfway up the hill.

I'm not doing the right thing, Heidi thought. But what is the right thing?

It was like a horrible test; an immense exam; she was failing; she had not worked her way through a single complete problem; people were dying and she was failing them.

I'm alone, Dear God, don't let me be alone!

Where are they?

*Make them come.*


*Saturday: 5:44* P.M.


Nobody was at the coffee shop. Patrick couldn't believe it. What was the matter with this town?

"Go hang out with kids your own age," said Noelle severely. Noelle knew everybody. She especially knew Patrick. She handed him a Pepsi as he left, winking. He winked back, although it embarrassed him; if Noelle had noticed that he could not manage coffee, had everybody else?

Okay, so now where did he go?

The girl he had been dating—if you could call it dating; the girl he usually met at things, and teamed up with, and had once kissed, but frankly he didn't think kissing was so great; of course if he had been less nervous it might have been . . . Anyway, that girl was kissing somebody else these days, somebody either more interested or less nervous, and he disliked running into her. She always gave Patrick a smile he could not interpret. He emphatically did not want to run into her.

So he drove around instead of trying to find the action.

Patrick loved driving. Loved roads. Loved cars. Among the many things Patrick wanted to do with his life was surround himself with vehicles. Anything with wheels. Anything with engines.

He loved the act of driving: every detail, from putting the key into the ignition to steering around tight corners. He loved keeping perfect track of the traffic around him, the traffic approaching, the traffic coming up from behind.

He loved the interior of his truck.

The accessories: the scanner that was always on; the radio that was always on softer, so he wouldn't miss any calls. He was dying for a car phone, but his parents simply looked amused when he brought it up. Patrick swore that when he had kids, he would never look amused.

It was his parents' only flaw, though.

The scanner sang the four electronic notes of Nearing River Emergency, and Patrick turned his radio down even softer to listen. Icy rain tapped gently on the hood, the windshield wipers shunted back and forth, the engine throbbed. To Patrick they were a symphony: the sound of a boy wrapped in a car with a big engine.

"Nearing River personnel, reported plane crash in the north end of town. Unconfirmed. Location, woods behind private home called Dove House off Rockrimmon Road off Old Pond Meadow."

It was Patrick's mother. Her voice was completely calm. "Ambulance and fire personnel await confirmation."

For Patrick, time did not include seconds and milliseconds. He did not debate choices. He just stepped on the gas and hauled hell for leather to Rockrimmon. He couldn't be but a mile from there. "Whooo-eee!" said Patrick out loud, laughing. I'll be first! he thought.

Rockrimmon was a very old road, but through a rocky, high area. Few houses had ever been built there. Putting septic systems and wells into those ravines and ledges was either impossible or horrendously expensive. The road, however, was wrapped in manmade stone walls. Two or three hundred years ago, some poor slob had actually tried to farm up here.

Old Pond Meadow had been widened so school buses could manage the curves. Rockrimmon had not been widened. It seemed to Patrick that there was somebody taking the bus from there this year, though. The road's name had come up at a meeting he'd attended with his parents, where they asked for Ambulance and Fire input on possibly widening Rockrimmon. It was one of those meetings meant to solve the world's problems, but they got bogged down in something pointless and never decided anything.

Patrick used the call-back frequency, but not his name. He did not say, "Hey, Mom, so exactly where is this place?" In his radio voice— he said, "Please identify driveway location on Rockrimmon."

Scanner listening was a big hobby in rural areas. That was one reason why you used codes on the air, so the entire world didn't know what you were talking about. 'Course, the entire world knew the codes, too, but still nobody ever said, "We're back at the barn and we put gas into the ambulance for the next run." They said, "We're 40."

Everybody would be listening. Men and women all over the area would be zipping up snow jackets, grabbing gloves, racing for their cars, turning on the de-icers, turning on the strobe lights and the sirens, and heading toward their fire and ambulance stations. For a call like this, it didn't matter whether you were signed up for duty or not; for a call like this, you were on duty.

His mother knew his voice, no matter how suave he tried to be, but she did not say, "Patrick! What are you doing over there, young man? You're supposed to be . . . "

She said, "It's exactly three eighths of a mile from the intersection with Old Pond Meadow. On your left. Two stone pillars and an open iron gate. Then a driveway also three eighths of a mile long."

His adrenalin was pumping like nothing he had ever felt before. He hardly needed a vehicle; he could have run as fast; he hardly needed an engine; his heart could have moved the truck. He would never need sleep or food again. Arrival first on the scene would satisfy him forever.

The stone gate appeared, and now he recognized it. Peacock Place, they used to call it, because several times in past years when the peacocks had screamed their horrible dying wails, neighbors had called in that somebody in the woods was hurt.

Patrick turned into the private drive. The first reality hit him and his heart sank. The drive was too narrow for two-way traffic. An ambulance could get in, but there would have to be traffic monitors to get it back out.

He was not going to be a traffic monitor. No way on earth. Let some other poor Junior do that.

Patrick flew into the courtyard and jammed on the brakes, skidding to a halt with a satisfying rubbery screech.

He felt as if he were in a foreign country, with this immense bricked expanse to park on, this cold and frozen fountain, this crazy shingled house with tiny glittering windows, like postage stamps on a gray page.

There was nobody there.

For a moment he was outraged; furious; homicidal.

It was a joke, a game he would kill whoever . . .

And then he smelled it: the fuel.

He heard it: the screams.

And he saw it: flames cresting the roof of the mansion.

Patrick jumped out of his truck and raced across the courtyard, losing his footing on the slippery brick. He hopped over a low stone wall and ran out onto the grass.

Below him lay the largest thing he had ever seen.

A huge plane.

Window after window after window: tiny rectangular black spots on an immense white body.

Like a Christmas card: gleaming white and winking colored lights.

For a moment Patrick could not identify why it did not really look like a plane. Then he realized that the section had no wing; the wing on his side had been torn away and was flaming hideously and noisily where it had fallen.

It was not the house that was on fire, nor was it likely to be. The distance was considerable and the ground between was rain-soaked.

Jet fuel, he thought. How many thousand gallons would they have on board? Depend if they were at the end or the beginning of the flight, I guess.

He remembered vaguely that you didn't use water on fires from fuel. But he was not trained in the Fire Department; he didn't really know anything about their techniques or equipment. Foam, he thought vaguely, and didn't know if Nearing River was equipped for that or not.

Patrick had never been in a plane. He was stunned by the size of the thing: not so much the length as the breadth: the circumference of the smashed plane was unbelievable.

Remaining sections of the vast plane were upright: so high up that Patrick could not believe that, either; they would need two-story ladders to get people out.

Other parts of the plane littered the landscape like a Beirut bombing.

And eerily, an overlay of silhouettes; people were walking around down there.

People lived through that? he thought.

Patrick forced himself back to the truck. His legs were weak. He hated himself for those weak legs. He picked up his scanner and struggled to think of institutionally correct things to say. Nothing came to mind. "It happened, all right, Mom," he said. "I think it's a 747. It fills the whole field. And some of the woods. We're gonna need everything we've got. It's bad. Some of it's already on fire."

"Right," said his mother, still calm. She made the calls without skipping a beat, including the Mutual Aid calls to every town in the area. If her son said they needed everything, she would call everything in.

Patrick left the truck, jumped over the stone wall again, and found himself with an elderly woman, obviously from the mansion, wearing a hooded, lined raincoat over a long pink bathrobe. She had forgotten about her feet and was still wearing fluffy little pink slippers. "Plane," she whispered, pointing. "It's a plane." Putting one hand over her mouth, she made little, contained barks of horror.

Patrick knew how she felt. No amount of training had prepared Patrick for this. Accidents happen one or two people at a time; a single car; a single heart attack; a single fall downstairs.

We're "the uh-oh squad," thought Patrick. We have absolutely no idea what to do except stand there and go *"uh-oh."*

Patrick had been trained as a First Responder. But he had never reached an accident or attended a patient without a crew of other, experienced people. He had never seen anybody who was burned.

Burned? thought Patrick. Incinerated.

He stared at the huge piece of plane and wing, which was the black center to screaming, frenzied flame.

He understood then what was screaming.

Not the fire.

*I'm First*, he thought, and for a moment he was entirely paralyzed.

# Six

Laura recognized the tone on Ty's scanner instantly: the electronic singsong of their own frequency. Although she had been a volunteer only four months, she slid right into rescue mode: her body stiffened, her ears pulled ahead of the rest of her senses, she tuned out the rock tapes being played, the laughter and the talk. She absorbed the dispatcher's voice.

"Plane crash," it said. "All units."

Patrick's mother was on, a very calm woman, a woman Laura admired and wanted to be exactly like.

"Rockrimmon Road off Old Pond Meadow," said Patrick's mother.

Laura raised her eyes, bringing sight back into her world. She and Ty were the only rescue-squad people at this party. She didn't even like Ty. Brains of a baked potato. "You have your truck?" she demanded. Of course he had his truck. A guy like Ty, he wasn't a man without his wheels.

"Come on," he said, "where's your coat?"

They didn't even remember the party; they were yanking on their coats as they dashed over the porch, down the steps. Ty's truck was blocked in by several cars.

"Plane crash!" whispered Ty, shaking his head. He didn't go back into the house to ask people to shift cars. He drove his truck right over the lawn instead, bumping over the curb and into the street. Ty loved doing stuff like that. Everybody suspected he was the one who did wheelies in the football field and ruined the turf each year, but nobody could prove it.

"Trucks," he said proudly to Laura, meaning every complimentary thing there was about vehicles that ordinary obstacles couldn't stop.

Ty's truck sported enough lights to dock the QE II: a row of blinkers on the top of the cab, an interior light that spun in circles, flashers attached to both headlights and taillights.

"All units," Laura told Ty, "does not mean you should signal outer space."

Ty hated girls who put down his pride and joy. If they hadn't been on the way to a crash, where duty called, he'd dump Laura by the roadside.

He didn't let himself get bogged down in irritation at Laura. I'm not going to be immature just because she is, he thought, pleased that he was better than she was. He rehearsed in his head, going over procedures, eliminating panic, questions, and fear.

They whipped past traffic that pulled over to the right for them. At two intersections, they met compatriots also rushing to the ambulance barn and the fire department. In a few minutes they were part of a veritable parade of volunteers.

"We're Juniors," said Ty briefly.

There was no need to amplify that.

Juniors ran the town by day. But it was night, and they would be elbowed out by every adult who showed up; and tonight, with this amount of excitement and desperate need, every adult was going to show. Adults that hadn't contributed a single hour in years were going to show. People whose training certificates had run out during the Reagan Administration were going to show.

Anger stiffened Laura. *Don't you butt in ahead of me just because you're older.*

I won't give them a chance, thought Laura. I'm going in no matter how old the people are ahead of me. So there.

Ty pulled into the correct entrance for the barn, so that departing ambulances wouldn't end up fighting opposing traffic just to leave their own barn. Laura leapt out of the truck even as Ty was looking for a parking space. The first ambulance had left, the rescue truck had departed, the paramedic's vehicle had left, but the second ambulance was still there, Laura raced over, praying to be the fourth, not caring in the slightest about Ty. She wanted a piece of the action, not a piece of hanging around hoping for a later ride.

"Fourth?" said the driver. He had the ambulance in gear, ready to roll; he was just waiting for a full crew. She could actually see the adrenalin behind his eyes, in the hand that gripped the wheel. A plane crash! They were all wildly excited.

"Fourth," said Laura, leaping in back.

The doors slammed, the ambulance pulled out, and Laura ducked her head down to keep from meeting Ty's eyes as she left him behind.

*Saturday: 5:44:30 P.M.*

Daniel could not tell how badly he was hurt. He knew only that he could not move. He sorted through the possibilities. He might simply be pinned down. Things were definitely resting on him. In that case, rescue workers would lift them off and Daniel would hop up and away.

On the other hand, he could not move his toes or his fingers. He might have a snapped spine. In which case he was paralyzed; he was going to be one of those people you saw on TV talk shows who had conquered their paralysis and played volleyball from their wheelchairs. He would never date, he would never sleep with a girl, he would never play baseball or sail a boat or even run in the door.

Tuck, he thought. *Where's Tuck?*

*Saturday: 5:45 P.M.*

Carly was still in the plane, still in her seat. Her seat had moved, however, as if it had never been bolted down. She was crushed between two large pieces of carpet; carpet lined with steel from the way it felt: horrible curling knife edges of metal had burst into her right arm. She could not bend her head enough to look down at her gut, but she could see that blood was slowly covering her knees. She could hear the rain, a civilized patter of normalcy, and if she raised her eyebrows really high she could catch a glimpse of the rain a few feet ahead of her.

I didn't die! thought Carly. Oh, wow. The plane crashed and I didn't even die. She wanted to tell the flight attendant. Guess what, Betsey! I did what you said and I made it!

Something soft lay in her arms. It took quite a while to figure out that it was Shirl's sweater. She hugged the sweater, pretending it was her sister. She held little conversations with the sweater, saying *everything will be all right now.*

The wind changed direction a little later and hurled some of the rain at Carly. She was terribly thirsty after all those peanut snacks and tried to tilt her face enough to drink the rain, but though it caught in her hair and diluted the blood on her knees, she could get none in her mouth.

No pain, but a lot of blood.

I'm in shock, thought Carly. I'll feel the pain later. I don't mind feeling pain later. I can hear people moving and working. We aren't all dead. Wherever we landed, help is coming.

She even smiled. It was still a good day. She was still going home. It was just going to take longer.

Carly hoisted her eyebrows and tilted her neck as much as possible. She regretted it. What she could see into was dripping.

Dripping water?

Or fuel?

As soon as the thought entered her mind, along with the thought came the smell. Fire. Somewhere there was a fire. Was it getting closer? Was that water in front of her? Or was it jet fuel, waiting for a spark?

Carly closed her eyes.

Just let it be quick, God, she said to Him. Just when it goes, make it go fast. Don't let me feel it. Please.


*Saturday: 5:46 P.M.*


There was a man at the top of the hill, standing with his legs spread and his hands on his hips. He had an official air of one surveying the scene. Mrs. Camp had come out and was standing next to him, plucking on his coat. Heidi ran up, thinking, He'll know what to do next.

But I know him, she thought. What's he doing here? He's in my study hall.

Her mind gave way, overloaded, and she skipped thinking about how somebody in her study hall was also an official on her hillside. "Heidi," she said to him.

He nodded. "Patrick."

It was weird, but his nod cleared her head.

Until the nod she had hardly been able to remember the location of her own house, but now her thoughts raced in logical rows: she was a computer. "I'll get us flashlights," she said, running to the back porch. The house was equipped with what her father called Invader Lights: spotlights in the gardens, in case they heard prowlers and wanted to expose them. Heidi flung the switches.

The rear hill lit up like a stadium.

The dogs were barking insanely. Winnie and Clemmie were like microphones with squeals. Fang was hurling himself against the door, trying to get out. She managed to keep all three dogs in while letting herself out, a triumph that occurred only a few times a year. Where's Tally-Ho? she thought, running back to Patrick and Mrs. Camp.

With the Invader Lights on, the crash was vividly outlined. It might have been machine guns over a period of years that had done all that damage. Metal debris, screaming victims, pieces of seats and human and tree. Immense curved plane divisions. By the reflecting pool lay a snowbank of airplane pillows.

Smoke, stinking and hideous, leaped like escaping souls from the burning wing.

*Saturday: 5:47* P.M.

His feet did not move.

Patrick was stunned. This could not be how he would react in a crisis: freezing up. He tried to take a deep breath and found that even filling his lungs was no longer a simple task. He forced himself not to imitate the horrible shocky noises the old woman was making. The girl Heidi was drenched, her ski jacket coated with ice, so she glittered like a rock star on stage. He took the flashlight from her, said, "Come on," although in fact she was already going, and then he was going, too, and once he took the first step he was fine. Action had begun.

Fear and fascination filled his veins, like some new kind of blood: a dizzying, whirling blood; he was transfused with it. A wild, clear excitement possessed him again: the adrenalin pump he'd gotten driving here: as if he were superman, could do it all, could do it forever.

In the woods where there was no fire, at least twenty people were up and walking around. Remarkably, an entire section of plane had landed rather easily. But from here, way below the house, the wrecked plane seemed horrifyingly close to the fire. The stench hit him like a blow to the head: nauseating, charred.

Patrick shouted, "Everybody who can walk, help somebody to the house! It's about two hundred yards out of the woods and up a grassy hill. You can see it as soon as you're out of the trees. Get in out of the rain and get warm. Help is on the way."

A woman took off her sweater and wrapped it around somebody's bleeding head, and then the two of them aimed for the house. A rather small man carried a similar-sized victim in his arms, like a newborn, apparently not noticing the weight. A big man in a sweatsuit and socks, no shoes at all, he must have taken them off to snooze comfortably while airborne, carried a young boy piggyback.

Patrick was able to get two people into the house very quickly. They were hardly hurt at all and used him like a conveyor belt. One was a woman who said she would make coffee, which struck Patrick as very peculiar: who would respond to a plane crash by perking coffee? The elderly woman in the pink slippers, however, was back inside, and she seemed to think that was an excellent idea. The women bustled away.

The other was a man who said he didn't like dogs, which also seemed to Patrick to be peculiar. What did dogs have to do with anything?

He had a sense of his mind being too full; he had to think of his mind as shelves, and allow only the important things to sit on them. Coffee and dogs he could cut. Patrick went down the hill again, and it was even more slippery; the treading feet had mushed the old wet snow into a ski slope. He ended up skidding on the other side of a large plane piece.

It was crushed and mangled, like a car run over by big-wheelies at the coliseum. Nobody in there could be alive. The ripped-open end of the plane had come together like jaws clenching.

At his feet lay a person, or what had once been a person.

Patrick sucked in air to stop himself from vomiting or weeping. Get up, get going, he willed himself. Don't think about this body, find somebody you can help.

Inches from his face hung a pair of dangling feet. Boys' white high tops. Brand-new. Not a single scuff. As he walked away, knowing that it too was dead, the feet swung. Whoever owned them was alive, trapped in a roll of plane.

Hanging onto plane pieces for support, Patrick curled himself up and around gaping, torn metal corners to see the tiny space where the victim lay. The space was so narrow it did not seem as if a magazine could have escaped being crushed, let alone a human. Then he saw that the passenger had not escaped being crushed. It was a boy, his own age or a little younger. That could be me, thought Patrick. The boy caught Patrick's hand. The fingers were so bony: Patrick felt as if a skeleton were clenching his hand, a person already dead and buried.

"Help is coming," said Patrick. "We'll have you out in a jiffy."

But there was going to be no "jiffy" here. Getting this kid out would be a terrible job. They'd have to peel back entire plane walls.

I wished for this, Patrick Farquhar thought. I drove around half an hour ago and wished that a really decent emergency would happen. "I'm Patrick," he managed to say. "What's your name?"

"Daniel."

"I'll get somebody down here right away, Daniel," said Patrick, thinking. Yeah, like who? Where are they? What are they doing?

He knew what they were doing. They were still driving from their homes to get to the rescue vehicles; rescue vehicles with full crews were still driving around the twisting narrow roads, trying to find the driveway in the dark.

"Hang in there," said Patrick cheerily, as if the boy had a choice; as if the boy had been thinking of watching a little TV instead.

But he could not stay. There was nothing he could do for Daniel. He had to go to somebody he could actually move to safety.

Daniel's hand tightened, keeping him there.

Patrick removed his hand anyway. He thought he had never done anything so cruel, so cold. He was careful not to look into the boy's eyes, because if he did, he could never sleep again. He was abandoning this kid. Patrick was almost sorry he had asked Daniel's name. It was better not to have a name if you were going to walk away.

It was called triage. The art of helping people who could be helped, and the terrible moral decision of walking away from those who could not.

Patrick said, "I'll be back."


*Saturday: 5:50 P.M.*


Teddie decided not to look at her leg again.

She also decided not to use her ears again.

The screams all around her were so horrible, like nothing she had ever heard before. Like a hundred nightmares, in which everybody woke up screaming, wanting their Mommy.

Teddie buried her face in Bear and sobbed. "I want my Mommy, too."

She opened her hand and peeked to be sure she still had her quarter.

The Band-Aids were flapping, attached only on one side. They were not catching the blood that covered her hand. Teddie hated blood. She wiped it off on Bear, but that was a terrible decision; now she could not bury her face in him; he was ruined.

The quarter was gone.

"My quarter," said Teddie. "I can't call Mommy."

She called Mommy anyway. "Mommy!" sobbed Teddie. "Mommy, come and get me!"

A woman moved an entire plane seat off Teddie, which helped a lot, but the woman did not stay to help. Teddie tried to run after her, but she couldn't move. "Mommy, come and get me!" Teddie shrieked over and over.

It was not Mommy who came. It was a big man. He said, "Let's get you inside where it's warm, okay?"

"Okay," said Teddie. Then when he touched her, she screamed again, "Mommy! Mommy!"

"Where does it hurt?" said the man.

Teddie said, "I dropped my quarter."

"I'll get you another one," said the man. He was kneeling, and then his hands were under her and he was picking her up, infant-style, so she sagged like a hammock across his arms. It hurt her so much that she screamed "Mommy!" over and over and over.

"It's okay," said the man. It did not reassure Teddie that the man was crying now. "It's okay," he said, though it obviously wasn't.

He fell down on the ice, and she screamed again, reliving the entire crash in the few inches of this second fall. She turned Bear around to a clean side, and stuck her face back into Bear.

"Sorry," the man said to her, "I'll slow down. What's your name?"

"Mommy," said Teddie instead, getting the man's priorities in order.

"I'll go back and get Mommy next," said the man.

"She's not here," said Teddie. "She's waiting for me. That's my quarter, to call her."

"I'll call her," the man promised. "You don't need the quarter anyway. It's not a pay phone."

They were inside.

It was a house. It was not a plane. It was warm. It was not raining anymore.

The man handed Teddie over to a woman in a bathrobe, a fluffy one, like grandmas wear. Teddie screamed when they passed her around. Then she said, "I'm sorry about all the blood."

"That's okay, honey, don't you worry. Now, what you and I are going to do here is fix this poor old leg. Let's lie down on this couch and see where we start."

*Saturday: 5:51 P.M.*

The nightmare of rescue overwhelmed Patrick.

Even assuming rescue trucks could get down that narrow, stone-walled driveway, there was no town water out here for fire trucks to tap; no hydrants. How could they fight a fire? Even if they got around the house and broke free of that courtyard, the slope would skid every piece of equipment into the wreckage.

As for the ambulances, even if they did get down the hill, they'd never get back up without a tow.

Which meant carrying every single wounded body out of the woods, up the hill, through the house, and out to the courtyard . . . where, unless they had a terrific traffic management plan, the ambulances could never get out again to reach the hospital anyway.

If it was indeed a 747, there could actually be *four hundred people* needing backboards and stretchers.

Or body bags.

The next nightmare was the icy rain, pelting down on injured passengers who were of course not wearing coats. So they'd freeze if they didn't burn. The ice made everything slippery. Its only possible benefit was to damp the fire out, but if there was another fuel tank, rain wouldn't have much effect on the explosion. Just add sizzle.

However, there were some good things. The house was immense. The heat was on; plenty of room to get warm, lie down, be treated. Phones and lights and electricity were available.

He helped an elderly woman who did not seem to speak English. She patted his face desperately, repeating syllables that meant nothing to Patrick. Patrick thought the only thing that could possibly be worse than being in a plane crash was to be in a plane crash in a foreign country.

Heidi set off through the woods, getting whiplashed cheeks from low twigs. She was carrying every coat and jacket in the entire coat room by the front door, and that was a great many. Her parents were fond of clothing. The first woman to whom she gave protection from the rain was trapped by a tree whose branches, on impact, had pierced the ground like so many stakes, and the woman was not going anywhere until somebody with a chainsaw arrived.

"Oh, wow," said the woman, quite cheerfully, considering the inhuman angle at which her right leg lay. "A mink coat," she said. "I used to be against furs, but what the hell."

She and Heidi even laughed.

Heidi gave out another coat and hit an obstacle.

A large group of victims were on the other side of one of the many tiny ravines that filled these woods. The ravine was probably only four or five feet deep, and only six across, but icy water slithered over the rocks; there was nothing to hold onto; she could not both carry coats and cross the ravine. She was not sure she could cross the ravine at all, let alone bring aid to those passengers.

Anyway, there was a person lying across the bottom.

Heidi had not known that she would recognize death, never having seen it for real. Death by plane crash, however, left visible tracks. It was not so much a person as mangled flesh. To cross the ravine, she'd have to step on him.

I can't, thought Heidi. I can't step on a dead—

Across the little ravine, hands were waved from the debris. Someone crawled toward her. The person could not see Heidi but crawled in a circular way, like a bird, with one wing.

Bridge, thought Heidi. I have to build a bridge. She tried to think of something . . . long and solid, something . . . light enough to carry down here.

*Saturday: 5:51:45* P.M.

Even in the smoky, stinking, icy air, Patrick could see that this girl passenger was stunning. He found himself glad that somebody so beautiful was not hurt, that she was walking around. "There's a boy back there caught under the wreckage. Go sit with him, okay?"

The beautiful girl looked at Patrick. Her eyes were immense, framed by a romantic cloud of hair that somehow was not touched by the rain, and in spite of the horror around him, Patrick was turned on.

But a hand touched his leg. A voice said, "Help me, I'm right here, please, there's something in me, something went right through me, please, please."

He forgot the beautiful girl, kneeling down to the horror of seeing some sort of metal rod going straight through the chest of a woman in a short-sleeved sweater. "I'm so cold," said the woman, and although he could not see her tears in the rain, he could tell she was crying.

Patrick took off his jacket, crying himself. He wanted to put it under her and protect her from the cold ground, but she could not be moved, so he tucked it over her, wrapping his jacket around the rod, saying, "Ambulances are coming. We'll have a stretcher down here in no time."

The woman smiled at him gently, and he could read her smile as if her lips spoke. *I have no time*.

From beyond the hill and the ravine came the wandering wail of the first siren.

Never had Patrick heard such a beautiful sound.

# Seven

Darienne could not believe that some filthy, mud-encrusted teenage boy was giving her instructions.

She had been standing there in an odd frozen position with interior noise she could not get rid of ricocheting inside her head. She had been knotting and unknotting her hands, counting the number of times she was doing it. She had the weird feeling of being asleep on her feet: walking alive through the nightmare of other people's dreams.

But now she was awake; that grimy boy touching her sleeve had brought her back to her senses.

She understood that phrase now: her senses really had abandoned her—thought, smell, vision, touch—but now they were back; Darienne was whole and wholly calm.

She walked carefully past the debris. She had to focus enough not to stumble, but she managed not actually to discern what lay on the ground. She even shut the noise out of her ears. When she came out of the wooded part, she could see the house clearly. Every light was on. How beautiful the place was against the night sky. It was also immense.

These people have money, thought Darienne with respect. Serious money. Old intensive-style money.

She wondered what kind of cars they drove.

She got up the slippery hill without stumbling and found a back door. A large copper red dog attempted to hand her a saliva-lathered latex toy. She kneed the dog away from her.

Firemen and ambulance people, policemen in uniforms, who-knew-what in special jackets were pouring through the house and out the back, like a tide. About time, thought Darienne irritably. She surveyed the scene.

Ugh.

Blood, mud, melting ice everywhere.

Antique rugs with a silken sheen were being ignored, and bleeding people were actually lying down on them. Darienne thought blood was the most disgusting thing in the entire world. She could not tolerate the idea of what the human body was like beneath the skin and felt strongly that as long as she kept her own skin flawless, she would never have to think about things like blood.

Shuddering, Darienne steered her way through the chaos into the kitchen. It was huge; semiremodeled from the days of many servants. Darienne shook her head, thinking of another age. She would have liked to be rich back then.

Darienne looked for a telephone. There should be one in the kitchen. There was, and it was in use. She waited impatiently for the man using it to finish up. The man appeared to be a doctor, talking of doctor-ly things. "I'm a cardiologist," he said into the phone, apologizing for choosing such a useless specialty. "I have no trauma experience. Patients are being moved without regard to technique. There's a danger of explosion and fire, and it seems wiser to shift the victims as fast as possible than to worry about spines and necks. We need stretchers down here."

Darienne thrummed her fingers on the counter. Was the doctor a passenger or a neighbor? He wasn't dressed right to be the owner of this house. She doubted that a mere cardiologist, no matter how successful, could afford this place. Unless he'd inherited it.

"It's a 747, and we were full," said the man, proving himself a passenger. "Several hundred people on board, therefore. There are a surprising number of uninjured; I'm going to guess ten percent are walking away. I'm setting up treatment in the house, which is huge. So we'll be able to keep patients warm and out of the rain, at least. But that's going to be pretty much my limit."

Darienne looked at her watch. Her wrist was unadorned. She must have lost it during the crash. Well, she would charge the airline for that.

"I don't know about landing a helicopter," said the cardiologist in his helpless voice. "The courtyard's out. There's a fountain in the center. The land behind the house slopes too much. There doesn't seem to be an owner here."

No owner here? thought Darienne, looking around with a bit more interest. She would have to check out the rest of the mansion.

"The local rescue people are arriving," said the doctor. "I'll have them call you." He disconnected.

Darienne picked up the phone immediately.

She called the airline to which she was expecting to transfer and requested them to bump up her flight. They wanted to know to which flight she wanted to be moved. Darienne was irritable. She didn't even know where she was, let alone how long it would take her to drive into the city. For all she knew she was in Pennsylvania, or Ohio, one of those inside states nobody cared about.

A woman took Darienne's arm. "We're setting up triage in the biggest room here. We're moving the furniture out into that long, thin hall so we can put the wounded flat on the floor. I need you to—"

"I'm busy," said Darienne.

The woman looked at her incredulously. "You're not hurt," she said, "you—"

"I'm busy," repeated Darienne, making another phone call. She turned her back for emphasis. It was unfortunate that all those people were hurt, but she was not. Darienne regarded this as a sign. She had been spared. She was worth more.


*Saturday:* 6:00 P.M.


Heidi's flashlight illuminated an oddly shaped open cardboard box. A lifesize baby doll was lying in it, clad in one of those knit one-piece suits. As she stepped over the box, the baby talked softly. Heidi stopped, legs straddling the cardboard, and stared down.

The baby was alive.

A woman in a military uniform said to her, "Papoose."

Heidi would have believed anything by now—Indian tribes, navy officers.

"Carry the baby up to the house, papoose box and all," said the woman. Heidi obeyed, resting the flashlight in the box with the baby. As the flashlight tipped, she saw that the military officer was wearing the name tag: *Betsey!*

"I'm one of the flight attendants," mumbled the woman. Some of her hair was no longer attached to her head. Blood streamed down that side of her face onto her shoulder. Heidi could not bear to look at it. "You come up to the house, too," said Heidi, wanting to clutch her own head in pain. "I'll get a towel or something." She wanted to press the scalp back down, stop it from looking so horrible.

"Later," said Betsey thickly. "Work to do. Flashlight," she added, taking Heidi's. Betsey stumbled over the debris toward the largest portion of the plane, the immense center, from which a rubber slide now extended. A small man crouched nervously at the top. So far up! Heidi was afraid of the height, and she was the one on the ground.

But they had to get out.

The fire in the torn wing actually roared. She had heard this description but had not known it would be true: like cars lined up to start a road race, motors roaring.

The flight attendant rallied, with what core of strength Heidi could not imagine, and began shouting encouragement. "Come on, it's fine, I'm here, slide on down, good work, keep moving!" The little man shot down toward her, and she caught him like a toddler on a water slide and set him upright. "Next!" called Betsey, like a cheerleader. "Get a rhythm here! I'm catching! We're doing good! Next! Come on! Next!"

They catapulted down. The slant was not for the faint at heart, and surely anybody who had just been through a plane crash was now faint at heart. In fact, she was amazed that the survivors hadn't followed up their crash with cardiac arrests.

Betsey turned, saw Heidi staring, and bellowed, like a trumpet in war, "Get that baby up to the house! Then come back down for more!"

Heidi rushed. The flight attendant had that kind of presence: I order, you obey.

She passed people sobbing, moaning, calling out in several languages. Saying, *Help me. I'm over here. Help me. Please help me.*

I can never move them all, thought Heidi.

Despair made her sob right along with them.

When she looked back over her shoulder, the extent of the carnage overwhelmed her.

*We can never do all this!* she thought.

The boy Patrick was suddenly next to her. He was carrying one end of a stretcher, and the person carrying the other end was a fireman. In uniform. The fireman wore an ugly yellow canvas-rubber sort of coat, the back of which read,

HARRIS
NEARING RIVER
VOLUNTEER FIRE DEPT

Help had come.

Help was here.

The 911 call had worked.

She had done the right thing after all.

"But we can't move everybody!" cried Heidi. Her pathetic thread of a voice drowned in the racket around them.

"It's like saving the world, honey," said the fireman, as he and Patrick passed her. "Nobody can save the world. But you can make up your mind to save one person. Now don't let your mind think on the size of this. Cripples you. Take that baby up and come down for another."


*Saturday: 6:10 P.M.*


Her quiet house, home to so few people, so rarely there, was full as if her mother were hosting a New Year's Eve gala.

She could not believe the number of human beings surging through her house.

It seemed hours ago that she had stood here alone, weeping and paralyzed. There was chaos inside the house, and yet it was orderly and it was not frightening. People were calmly doing their jobs, seeing a need, answering it. Somebody took the papoose box out of her arms.

Like a sleepwalker, Heidi passed through the Hall, crossed the Gallery, and stepped out her own front door. A maelstrom of lights, strobes, bullhorns, and flashers had turned the quiet courtyard into a fireworks celebration. Fire trucks were arriving. Ambulances were already here. Cars had poured into the courtyard. A row of pickup trucks had parked up against the low stone wall and trained their headlights to illuminate the crash site.

She looked down at her watch.

Half an hour since the plane came down, thought Heidi. I usually can't even get dressed that fast. And here in half an hour, I've saved lives, passed out coats, met rescuers.

Relief had barely lit Heidi's face when it vanished. The ambulances were ready to leave . . . but the lane was too narrow. *There was no exit.* As the cars and trucks of rescue workers poured up the driveway to Dove House, they then filled the lane.

What good is rescue if we have gridlock? thought Heidi. She stepped out into the courtyard, into the dizzying array of whirling blue and red and yellow and white lights, the men shouting, the women looking grim, the trucks unable to move. "Who's in charge?" she said.

"My dad is, actually," said Patrick. He did have a grin of relief and joy on his face, and it didn't vanish when he saw the traffic problems. The sight of his father steering a bunch of volunteers in a specific direction gave Patrick as much relief as Teddie would have had if her Mommy had arrived. Patrick said *"Dad"* in almost the same voice as Teddie would have, too. His father put an arm on his son's shoulder for just a moment.

"This is Heidi; she lives here," said Patrick. "She can tell you anything. Heidi, my dad, Mr. Farquhar."

Immediately she was surrounded by big demanding men. They wore firefighting gear, packs for emergency breathing strapped to their backs, big boots, helmets with thick plastic visors, immense gloves. "Is there another entrance? Another driveway? A neighbor close enough so we can come in through their driveway?"

"No. The woods are full of ravines. You can't cross them."

"Is there anywhere to land Life Star?"

"What's Life Star?"

"Hospital helicopter."

Heidi said, "What kind of landing space does that need?"

They told her.

She nodded. "Way out past where the wing caught fire is a pretty flat field. Six acres. When we had horses, we kept them there. It was mowed this fall to keep trees from growing."

"Great. Now. Is there any way around these stone walls in this courtyard? We've got to get this place opened up."

Heidi shook her head. Builders in New England, since building had begun in New England, were fond of stone walls, and many masons had worked many years around Dove House.

The man's jaw tightened.

Heidi hung her head, thinking. We should have dismantled those stone walls years ago.

She should have known that one day this would come up. It seemed to be her own fault for not planning ahead. The self-loathing that had crippled Heidi at boarding school weakened her again. She couldn't even meet their eyes. If the rescue effort failed, it would be because of her stone walls.

"Are your parents home?" asked another man sharply. She had a feeling he wanted to shake her.

They know I'm useless, thought Heidi. And I am. "They're out of town," she said. She was apologizing. It was wrong of her to have parents who were out of town.

The host of trucks, cars, ambulances, fire trucks, and rescue vehicles were stuck as if in a turnpike accident. They couldn't turn around any more than you could on a six-lane highway. As far as you could see, vehicles had stopped where they were blocked. Would-be rescuers were abandoning them, heading on foot for the crash site, thus doubling the problem: no drivers to move the vehicles if they ever did open up a path.

They're jerks! Heidi thought suddenly. It's their own fault! They should know better than to wreck their own exit.

She thought of the papoose baby, the little girl whose bone had stuck up out of her leg, the bleeding flight attendant soldiering on at the base of the broken plane. Heidi's brain started working again. "There are two possibilities. We can knock down the whole wall here, where the arch is—"

"No," said Mr. Farquhar. "We'd need a bulldozer, which we don't have."

"Then the hedge has to go." She led him beyond the courtyard, where a long row of ancient holly, beautiful beyond compare, was a vicious sentry. Her mother raided the hedge every December, filling the house, the local museum, and all the town's churches with green boughs and red berries.

"This is where the holly for St. Anne's comes from?" asked Mr. Farquhar.

Heidi shrugged. "Yes, but it's only holly. Chainsaw through the bottom of each trunk. Toss them into the ravine. From there you can drive down the hill," she pointed, "and taking care not to drive into the reflecting pool, you'll be at the bottom between the two parts of the plane crash."

"Right in the jet fuel," said another man. "I love driving over spilled jet fuel."

Mr. Farquhar studied the scene. "Can we get back up?" he said.

"It's pretty icy." Heidi brightened. "But you know what? We have a mountain of wood chips behind the barn. For mulching the gardens. Probably two or three dump-truck loads. You could move that over the slope to get traction."

Mr. Farquhar did not look happy about the prospect of moving two or three dump-truck loads of wood chips, one shovel at a time.

She said, "Or you could drive straight through the barn. If the plane had landed a few hundred feet uphill, it would have taken the barn down anyway. I bet if you got a big enough truck, revved that motor, and just kept going, you could bring the barn right down and—"

"I'll do it!" said Patrick eagerly.

Patrick's father laughed. "I like you, kid," he said to Heidi. "But we'll leave your barn standing."

Patrick was vastly disappointed. Heidi almost laughed herself to see the intensity of his expression. He had a nice face. She liked how it mirrored his father's. She liked a guy who wanted to drive a truck through a barn.

Mr. Farquhar, however, yelled for chainsaws and went after the holly.

In a moment, Patrick was gone, everybody in the courtyard was busy again, and Heidi again thought, But where's Tally-Ho?

*Saturday: 6:18 P.M.*

The ambulance crew had no way of knowing whether they would end up on an estate or in a trailer park. This part of New England was resistant to zoning; pockets of rural slum were not far from estates of famous actors, retired diplomats, and millionaire chairmen of boards.

Wealth divided Laura's mind. It was wonderful to look at; to gawk at; to think—so this is how they live. It was so nice to have around: stately white clapboard country mansions and magnificent stretches of green lawn.

But the same people often refused to pay their annual ambulance fee.

The same people often gave the worst tips to teenagers waiting table at local restaurants and were rude to teenagers who mowed their lawns.

She knew from the cute little bridge that this was estate country. And when she leapt out of the ambulance to take the first stretcher— it turned out to be the fifth stretcher, actually; other crews had beaten them to it—she recognized Dove House.

The girl who lived here was in Laura's gym class. Laura had plenty of friends; she didn't need another; she had never spoken to Heidi Landseth. Heidi wouldn't stay in public school anyway; she belonged at Miss Porter's or Ethel Walker or one of the other hoity-toity prep schools in Connecticut.

Laura and her crew ran toward the plane crash but never even rounded the side of the house; never even saw the downed plane at the bottom of the hill; the first wounded victim was carried up to them by two walking wounded passengers.

The man was burned. Laura had never seen burns before. Never smelled them. The stench coated her tongue, invaded her gut. She was going to get sick, she knew it. The woman carrying the other end of the stretcher said sharply to Laura, "Breathe through your mouth." Laura steeled herself not to get sick, not to faint.

He also had a sucking chest wound. Every time he breathed it sounded as if he were underwater. They fitted a cervical collar around his neck, they put MAST trousers on his legs to prevent shock, they sealed the open chest wound, and gave him oxygen. The senior crew member started an IV. Laura was not trained for that.

The ambulance could take two victims, although Laura had never been in an ambulance with both stretchers filled. Now she saw how hard the ride to the hospital was going to be. The crew would hunch over, doing what little they could to stabilize their two badly hurt patients. She was proud of herself; she had not gotten sick; she was doing the right things in the right order.

Now it was up to the driver.

But the driver did nothing.

They went nowhere.

The exit was blocked.

*Saturday: 6:22 P.M.*

Patrick had finished his training a year and a half before. They had had a textbook just like any other textbook: chapters with questions at the end, plenty of photographs with captions, some graphs, an index. Although there were frequent update training sessions, he had not looked at the textbook once since then. But he could see the page of high-impact accidents as if somebody were holding it open before him. The color photographs had made him gag when he first saw the book.

Now, at his feet, lay a man whose arm looked as if it had been pushed down in a blender. Now Patrick knew that the book illustrations were clean and neat, meant for inexperienced eyes. "Help," whispered the man. Patrick and a team of ambulance people—people he didn't even know; people who had come Mutual Aid from a neighboring town—knelt to slide the man as gently as possible onto a stretcher.

The textbook had said simply that high-impact injuries, whether from velocity, like a car crash, or height, like a plane crash, meant multiple long-bone fractures, plus head, neck, back, and chest injuries. Patrick had not quite grasped that each victim might have all of those. That it would be visibly, horrifically gory.

They had had Disaster lectures in EMT training. It had been pretty exciting. He remembered when the instructor had passed around samples of the Disaster tags. When you had only one or a few victims, which was certainly all Patrick had ever had, you didn't need tags, but when you had hundreds, somebody somewhere had to decide who went into the ambulance first, and who waited for the next trip; who got a doctor next . . . and who didn't. Every hurt passenger would be tagged for identification by the ambulances lined up in the court-yard. On top of the tag, you could write down the vital signs, like pulse and respiration. Below the space were large brilliantly colored strips: the bottom color was the one that counted.

Red—Stop and get this guy; you can save him if you go fast

Yellow—Slow; this guy can wait a little

Green—Go past: he'll be okay on his own

Black—He's dead

Patrick had not realized that—in this plane crash at least—when you divided patients up into the traditional color categories—you could eyeball it.

This guy was a Red.

The tags would be tied to buttons or sleeves, and the color panels could be ripped off if the patient's condition changed. If this patient stopped being a Red, they'd rip off the Red panel. Then his tag would be Black. During training the kids had squealed with giggly horror at the symbols that went along with each color. Yellow was a turtle. Red was a rabbit. But Black—Black was a shovel.

Stay Red, Patrick thought at the man. Stay Red, he thought at God.

He and two of the team log-rolled the victim onto the stretcher, while very gently a fourth man braced the damaged arm with a folded blanket. Then they strapped the man tightly into the stretcher, so his weight would shift as little as possible as it slanted, going up the hill.

Trying not to slip, the taller of the volunteers carried the lower end and tried to keep it high, keep the poor man as flat as possible. There was a feeling of frenzy among all the teams moving patients: there was still fire several hundred yards away; there could be another fire right here, right where they stood. Speed counted. Getting to the house counted. Having to go slowly on the icy patches made them all want to scream.

Patrick remembered the Golden Hour. (His mother was partial to that phrase: it reminded her of the Golden Rule. Patrick didn't see the similarity.)

Since the Korean War, emergency treatment staffs had known that physiologically, the human body could care for itself for even the worst wounds for about an hour. If you could keep that victim's airway open and stop his bleeding—if you could do that *and* get him to the hospital within one hour, you could probably save him. Even if he were very badly hurt.

But with the worst patients, you had only an hour.

Sixty minutes.

You couldn't say—"Hold the clock; we have to wait for the ambulance!"

You couldn't say—"Hang on, fella; we gotta wait till somebody cuts away the plane before we get you out."

You couldn't say—"This isn't fair; we have to cope with a hill and some ice; give us more minutes this time."

The clock ticked, and the Golden Hour ran out.

If you had only one victim, say a motorcycle accident, and a crew of four to rescue, an Hour was not a difficult thing. Even way out here in the woods, you could get your victim to a hospital in time. Say, three minutes until the accident's called in; say, five minutes to get a volunteer to the ambulance barn and another five to get the ambulance to the scene; plus the time it actually took to get the victim onto a backboard, into the ambulance, and leave; plus fifteen minutes to reach a hospital . . . you could make it.

But say the victim was in a car and couldn't be cut free for another quarter hour. Say other drivers didn't make way for your ambulance; or the weather was terrible and you had to drive slowly; or you got to the hospital and they were already handling two other accidents and your patient had a wait ahead of him . . .

Your Hour was up.

Or rather, the victim's Hour was up.

Panting, fingers stiff with cold, they reached level ground and went on in the door being held open for them, carefully maneuvering the stretcher through Heidi's house and out into the courtyard again, into the blaring, blinding lights.

All these people.

All these hurt people.

Sharing the same Golden Hour, the same precious sixty minutes.

# Eight

*Saturday: 6:26 P.M.*

The rain came down onto Carly's cheek. At first it was just cold and awful, but it began to hurt, as if slowly taking her skin off and getting down to the nerve cells. After a while her face hurt more than anything; it was the icy rain that was going to kill her. She could not bear the rain on her face. Just cover my face, she thought.

But she could not seem to call out.

*Saturday: 6:27 P.M.*

Ty could have killed Laura. The names he would like to call that girl were short and suitable.

Inside the barn he put on his orange slicker, with NEARING RIVER RESCUE SQUAD written on the back, and his last name, MARONN, below that. He hated his last name. Laura was not the only one to change the first vowel and call him Moron. Ty donned the hard hat with the cowboylike rim and hoped for a run to join.

He hoped wrong. The plane-crash call had brought out of the woodwork dozens of grown-ups who were rarely active these days, but who, like Laura, were going to the head of the line and leaving Ty in the gutter.

He shrugged, got back in his truck, and headed for the site.

A full mile from Rockrimmon, he hit traffic.

There were already so many volunteers pouring in from every town within reach, and so many bystanders pouring in from what looked like half the nation, that there was no going anywhere.

Ty didn't want to get caught in it.

He pulled into the closest driveway, parked in some stranger's turnaround, locked the truck, grabbed his heavy-duty flashlight, got out, and began running.

He was going to be part of this rescue if it included marathons.

He ran the mile easily, slipping in the slush of the road but not quite falling; jumping between stalled cars when opposing traffic made it pretty stupid to be in the middle of the road.

He reached the intersection of Old Pond Meadow and Rockrimmon.

Rockrimmon was two lanes, but barely. Timid and beginning drivers were quite sure it was only one lane.

The first ambulance was trying to leave but no longer had space to get out. Fire trucks trying to arrive filled the incoming lane. Parked cars and trucks of people who had decided to walk in filled the outgoing lane. Nobody was going to get rescued. They were just going to form a major traffic jam and sit the night out.

A row of five fire trucks filled the eastern direction down Old Pond Meadow. Backing those huge vehicles up in the dark, on the ice, past the curving stone wall—poor idea.

But west, the way he'd run—it was possible.

Ty beckoned the ambulance toward him, recognizing the driver: a fat old guy he'd never liked, a know-it-all who lorded it over the teenagers and grasped every bit of knowledge to himself instead of teaching.

Ty could hardly stand it that this slob was in the action and Ty was going to direct traffic.

He put his feelings out of his mind. Over and over in training, they'd said, You can't stuff your head with personal things; think procedure; get the job done. Period.

He tapped on the closed driver's window of the car closest to him. "Pull in closer to the stone wall. I'll direct you." The driver obeyed him, and a precious three feet were gained. Ty ran to the next car, whose owner gave him a second flashlight, and the next car, and the next, wedging them forward and off to the side, giving the ambulance room.

They met, of course, an oncoming ambulance trying to pass the stalled traffic; normally an intelligent decision, but not this time. Ty backed and ordered and wedged and pointed and finally got passing room for the existing ambulance.

His feet were soaked through.

He put that out of his mind.

He worked his way back the entire mile to his truck, getting people out of the road, forcing people to listen to him, setting up traffic directors at every intersection—there weren't many; only three on this entire backwoods section—until finally, an entire twenty minutes later, he had gotten the road clear for the ambulance.

*Twenty minutes.*

It made him sick.

Who died during that twenty minutes? What precious life bled away because of cars littering the road like so many useless soda cans?

But Ty understood the drivers. He too wanted fiercely to be on the site. He wanted to be part of *that* action, not this action. What was this? It was running vertical parking lots in the dark.

They also serve who only run and park, Ty said to himself. He entertained himself with thoughts of murdering Laura.

He got a lot of flak. The newcomers were from the State, they were from the Region, they were from Disaster Control, they were doctors, they were nurses, they were neighbors.

"Walk in," said Ty firmly to each one. How he envied them. They'd get there eventually.

Me, I'll just stand here for eternity, parking cars. I don't even get tips.


*Saturday:* 6:35 P.M.


The rain stopped.

Heidi had never been so grateful to the sky.

She held up her palms to test her conclusion. The gesture was being repeated all over the grounds of the estate.

We are like primitive people praying to the gods of weather, Heidi thought. Human beings from time immemorial, ancient Sumerians and Egyptians, ancient Indians and Vikings, held their hands like this. O Sky, relent! Give us a break!

Instead of waving flashlights they should be holding the holly branches and gathering their offerings at some great hearth.

*But there is a great hearth here,* thought Heidi.

Momentarily she watched a girl about her own age, in an ambulance jacket, along with two others getting a backboard under a patient. Now they strapped the patient carefully onto a stretcher. While the girl took the patient's pulse, the other two worked plastic trousers up on the victim's legs and then inflated them. She did not know what that was for, what it did, what it was called. Around the patient's head they placed two heavy orange slabs, rather like a swimmer's life jacket, and strapped the head securely down.

Heidi was jealous.

It's my yard, she thought, and I can't even take a pulse. I don't even know what to feel, or where to feel it, or what to count.

And then she remembered something. Something really important.

Dolt, dolt, dolt! she accused herself. How could you be forgetting that? You're such a worthless fool, Heidi.

She tore around the grounds, looking for Mr. Farquhar.

So many people. So much commotion. And everybody so formless, so faceless, in their huge, enveloping fireman's coats: just big, moving, yellow blotches. She wanted a bull horn, she wanted a microphone, she wanted Mr. Farquhar.

Of course when she found him, he was busy. There were two men and a woman arguing with him, or giving him facts, or just generally yelling. Heidi could not tell. He could hardly believe it when she interrupted him. It was only because she owned the house and the land that he could even bring himself to spare her two seconds. He faced her momentarily, holding in his annoyance, the whole tilt of his head saying—Make it quick, girl, I have better things to do.

"The fire," said Heidi. "We have a dry hydrant, Mr. Farquhar. My father had it put in when we built the stables, in case we had a fire from the hay or something."

Everybody with Mr. Farquhar spun around at the phrase. Breathless half smiles decorated their faces, as if getting Christmas presents. How often the comparison to Christmas had come to her in this horrid hour: the sparkling lights, the happy gasps.

They would need two thousand feet of five-inch hose. They would attach it to the never-used hydrant her father had installed at the pond, in case of emergency.

*In case of emergency.*

I guess this is the case, Dad, thought Heidi. And she looked at all the faceless people who had made her feel so rotten because of her courtyard and her stone walls. So there, she thought. We have a dry hydrant. So there.

*Saturday: 6:40 P.M.*

Daniel's legs were buckled up in such a gruesome position he could not look at his own body. It hurt horrifyingly. Right after the crash he had not seemed to have pain. He had just hung there. Then the pain hit, and he screamed for quite a while, and now for quite a while he had stayed quiet. People kept saying to him, "We're coming, son, we're coming."

It was amazing how many voices said he was their son.

A fat woman was sitting with him now. She had a funny little canteen thing with a long curving straw out of which Daniel could drink water. It took a lot of effort to sip from such a long straw. But the fat woman couldn't get it closer to his mouth. "What's your name, honey?" she said to him.

"Daniel." He knew she was fat because he could see her folded feet. She was wearing a skirt and had very thick ankles and even thicker navy blue shoes. He didn't know what she was sitting on. He couldn't see her face, either. She couldn't twist up inside his prison the way that first boy had.

"I have a grandson named Daniel, honey. I like that name. Are you traveling alone, Daniel?"

He shook his head, and great splinters of pain, like flying metal, pierced him. "My brother," he said at last. "Tuck. He was on the plane, too. He's only thirteen."

"He's fine," said the woman. "He's up in the house."

Daniel wondered how she knew. He wondered if she was just saying that to comfort him. If it was a lie. "He was here with me," said Daniel. His lips were very thick. Had he hit his face causing his mouth to swell up?

"You're kind of wrapped in the plane, Daniel. But we're going to cut you out real soon, honey."

He noticed that she did not give him details on Tuck.

Daniel said to her, "Am I dying? Who are you? Will you tell my mom?"

She could not reach him very well. He felt her kiss on his lower arm. "I'm Mrs. Jemmison," she said. "I'm a nursery-school teacher. I have a nursery school in my home, about three miles from here, Daniel. My husband and I are both ambulance volunteers, although we haven't been active this year. We heard the call come over the scanner, and we got in the Buick and hauled over."

He thought, If she kisses me, that means I'm dying. This is it. Oh, well, at least I don't have to worry about being a paraplegic.

Daniel wanted to cry so much that oddly enough he had control over it and decided not to. Mrs. Jemmison would be the one who told his mom and dad how he died, and he was not going to have Mom and Dad think he whimpered. "How will they cut me out?" he said, thinking mechanical thoughts to keep away the death thoughts.

"They've got the Jaws of Life. Those are sort of hydraulic scissors that cut through anything, Danny boy. Even planes."

His mother hated it when anybody shortened his name. She loved the name Daniel and detested the name Danny. But he didn't correct Mrs. Jemmison. He wanted her to stay right here. Somehow he felt dying would be easier if he had company.

"You're going to be the big excitement of the night, Daniel," said a man's voice from beyond Mrs. Jemmison.

"Tell them not to save me for last," said Daniel, and he and Mrs. Jemmison laughed.


*Saturday: 6:41 P.M.*

"To cross that ravine," said Patrick, "we need a makeshift bridge."

"There are ladders in the garages," suggested Heidi. "Maybe if we laid a ladder flat and put boards over the steps so we don't fall through . . ."

They were already winding through the crowd in the courtyard to the garages. The buildings were locked. Automatic door openers clipped to the sunshields in the family cars opened these doors. Heidi herself rarely drove. For some reason, it had never appealed to her. Now she was mad at herself for that, too. Why hadn't she known she would need her own set of keys? Her own way in? "Back in a second," she said to Patrick.

Heidi ducked through a crowd of people off-loading backboards from a visiting ambulance and ran into the large pantry between the kitchen and the back porch. From the wall she took Burke's immensely full spare key ring. Each key, thank goodness, was neatly labeled. Otherwise they'd have been there half an hour, stabbing away at the garage keyhole.

In the garage were two good ladders. "The aluminum one," said Patrick instantly, lifting it off its pegs. Heidi took one end, expecting him to take the other, but he said, "No, it's light enough for you to carry yourself. Get it down there and get it in place. I'll look for boards to lay across it." He helped her angle it through the doors. "Is there a workshop?" He asked. "Woodworking?"

She shook her head. "Burke does that at his house, the gatehouse; it's a half mile down the lane."

He stared at the key chain, as if hoping it would suggest solutions.

Heidi said, "How about the barn? Take a door right off a horse stall. They're on hinges; you could just lift one out."

"Brilliant," he said. "I love you, Heidi."

She slithered down the hill. A woman she had never seen before, with white hair and fragile ankles, took one end of the ladder. "What are we doing?" said the woman. She was old. Blue veins stood out on her age-spotted hands.

"Making a bridge," said Heidi.

The two of them worked easily together, Heidi in the ravine, ice water sloshing over her feet, until the ladder was in place. "Stabilize it with river rocks," said the woman. The rocks were unbelievably heavy. Heidi felt as if she were shifting continents. But she got two rocks moved where she needed them, just as two men—neither of them Patrick—came down with a horse-stall door. It took two doors, actually, and by now there were so many people assisting that one took up a permanent position as ladder-bridge supervisor, calling out, "Put your weight dead center, don't step on the edges, go slow, put your foot here, now you've got it."

Heidi yearned to be the one supervising. But she didn't know anything.

The elderly woman said to Heidi, "Your feet are soaked. Go into that big house up there and get your feet dry." Heidi protested that she was fine, but the woman gave her a piercing look: the kind that really good teachers have: *Move it or die, kid.*

So Heidi ran back to the house to get boots.

She was amazed to find she was not slipping.

There was no longer ice or even grass on the hill.

Four women were hauling a canvas sheet covered with wood chips and dumping it to make a very wide path up to the house and a second path to the archway that led to the courtyard. They dumped their load of mulch, turned around, and crossed the hill for more.

Heidi had no idea who they were. It gave her such a warm feeling that these hills, where she knew no neighbors, were in fact full of neighbors: of good people hurrying to help.

Back in the house, kicking off her icy sneakers, she rubbed her feet dry and ran up to her room for boots. She tugged socks on over her bare feet, swelling up now that they were warm, and jammed them into the boots just in time. Another minute and they would have been too swollen to cram in.

They'll need more blankets downstairs, she thought.

She went down the hall toward Mrs. Camp's wing, planning to raid the linen closet there because it was full of old blankets nobody used anymore.

Mistake; big mistake. The dogs leapt out on top of her, barking insanely. Winnie and Clemmie headed for the stairs, while Fang stood up on his hind paws and began licking her to death. Heidi shoved Fang back in, slammed the door, and raced through the house trying to gather up stupid, worthless Winnie and Clemmie.

She skidded past people carrying coffee trays and bandages and IVs. Her stupid, worthless semidogs cut between ankles and slipped yippily out of her grasp. I must look like a total jerk, thought Heidi. How humiliating. "Sorry," she kept muttering. She was actually blushing. Hoping that at least Patrick would not see her.

Now she could smell bacon frying. I'm demented, she thought. Bacon?

In her kitchen, older people who could not toil outdoors were calmly running a canteen, making sandwiches and coffee, heating soup.

She found Clemmie there, yapping for bacon, picked the wretched hairball machine up, ran back upstairs, and threw Clemmie into Mrs. Camp's room again, only to have Fang slip back out.

It did not help the atmosphere in the lower hall when a huge, galumphing dog raced joyfully toward wobbly survivors, and a girl at the top of the stairs shouted, "*Fang!* Down!"

*Saturday:* 6:55 P.M.

Patrick meant to join the firemen.

They had divided into two groups: those putting out the fire on the detached wing and those rescuing passengers stuck high in the rest of the plane.

Driving down the hill proved to be impossible, so instead, they detached the immense ladders from their trucks and carried them. They were now removing from the plane passengers who had not been thrown free and were too badly hurt to use the rubber slide. Most were badly injured, and each transfer to a backboard or stretcher was scary and hard. But it was nothing compared to lowering the stretchers back down the ladders to the ground.

Plus, everybody who remained conscious was afraid of the fire. The wind tossed sparks from the burned plane section, which crackled now and then, threatening like a volcano. Although a stream of water was now showering the wing, it wasn't out yet. And there had to be more fuel in other tanks.

Everybody's stomach was clenched with the desire to hurry, hurry, hurry, hurry—get out of here—get the victim out—get myself out, too.

A man who appeared to be completely unhurt kept walking back and forth screaming. There was something machinelike about his screams: he was rhythmic, as if supplying backup for a rock band.

He's in shock, thought Patrick.

The man's screams were unbearable, and yet Patrick did not want to waste time escorting an unhurt man to the house, calming him down, putting him indoors, getting his feet up to get the blood back to his head and heart. Not when there were people dying all around.

But the screaming went on and on until Patrick gave in, and, shuddering against the impact of the man's screams, dragged him up to the house saying, "It's okay, it's okay," which was probably the stupidest thing he had ever said in his life.

*Saturday:* 6:59 P.M.

Chainsaws screamed.

Carly thought the worst punishment of all was that shrieking metallic whirr buzzing through her mind, her teeth, her bones.

She was bleeding.

Strangely enough, there was no pain. Just fear, fear that came in surges, like aftershocks from earthquakes, rippling through her and bringing her to the edge of vomiting. Each time, she managed to stop herself. She knew that she was passing in and out of consciousness.

People were working all around her.

Sometimes somebody patted her shoulder or her hair or her hand. "We're coming," voices kept saying, "we're coming, you hang on."

She wanted to answer them, but she had no voice. She was still inside herself, she knew that, but talk was something she no longer did. Still as Carly lay, she was spinning in circles.

I'm out of time, thought Carly. I'm seventeen and out of time.

The whirling effect spun her gently out of herself, and for a while her eyes closed; the scream of sirens and saws ended. A light as bright as bombs penetrated her skull.

She opened her eyes, thinking this might be heaven or hell. But it was still a plane crash. They had brought floodlights, and one was trained on her. She tried to tell them that it was blinding her; that she had no way to turn her head. She wanted to say, "Get my sunglasses, they're in my bag." She wanted to make a joke. "Hey, you guys, darken up there."

But it was not the world that darkened.

It was Carly, growing slowly less attached, less aware, less alive.

Shirl, she thought, Shirl, I'm sorry. Don't be mad.

"We're coming, honey," said a voice, or several voices. A chorus of echoes rang in her head. *We're coming, honey, we're coming, honey, I'm going home, Shirl, I'm coming, honey.*

Her sense of what was going on grew thinner and thinner, narrower and narrower, dizzier and dizzier.

This is what it means, thought Carly, to hang onto life by a thread. I am not attached by jugular vein or pumping heart of spinal column. I am attached by a thread.

*Saturday: 7:00 P.M.*

This is so ridiculous, thought Heidi. I'm exhausting myself more fetching dogs than saving lives.

She finally cornered Winnie in the front hall, barking death wishes at a tall, slim, beautiful girl using the hall phone.

"A taxi," the girl was saying with intense anger. "I want a taxi at this address. What do you mean, you can't get here? This is where I am."

A man in a fireman's uniform tapped the girl on the shoulder. "We need the phone."

The girl shrugged off his hand irritably, glaring at him.

"There are no taxis in this town," Heidi explained, trying to catch Winnie. Winnie escaped between the beautiful girl's beautiful legs. This was definitely a person on whom clothes hung perfectly. This was the kind of girl her roommates had expected for a roommate.

The girl looked Heidi up and down. Heidi had not felt so rejected since boarding school. How could this girl be neat under these circumstances? How could her hair be sparkly and her scarf at a jaunty angle? She had to be a passenger. She looked as if she had suffered no more trauma than a paper cut.

She looks as if she's the one who lives here, thought Heidi.

"I need the phone," said the fireman sharply.

"I'm using it," said the girl, even more sharply.

For a moment Heidi and the fireman waited their turn.

Then Heidi said to him, "Why are we being polite?" She put her finger on the phone buttons and disconnected the girl. "Give him the phone," she said.

"Who do you think you are?" said the girl, furious and imperious.

"I'm the owner of the phone," said Heidi. "And I say the firemen use it first. How come you're not in the back helping?"

The fireman savagely punched his numbers.

"Because I have a plane connection to make," said the girl.

The fireman and Heidi looked at each other in perfect harmony, and for once in her worthless little life, Winnie did a good deed.

She bit the beautiful girl's ankle.

# Nine

Flight #116 was really quite late, but people accustomed to meeting planes didn't get worked up about it. So what else was new?

They heaved large sighs every time they looked up at the arrival-time screen, as if hoping airline personnel would be humiliated by all this sighing and quickly land the plane.

It was not a strategy that worked.

Teddie's parents were laughing. They had walked back to one of the wall pay phones and called Gramma and Poppy. The details of Teddie's departure had delighted them.

"I can't wait to see that quarter taped to her palm," said Teddie's mother. "Let's get her hand on the camcorder. Our daughter's first solo air flight, complete with Mickey Mouse Band-Aid assist."

"I wish there was a place where I could film the plane actually landing," said Teddie's father, circling a row of chairs for at least the hundredth time. He had enjoyed the two weeks alone with his wife while Teddie visited her grandparents. Yet it had been a long two weeks. Maybe next year they would make it one week. When you had only one child, you needed all the child time you could get.

Come on, plane, he thought irritably, get a move on.

Near them, a child bounced around, zinging with sugar energy. The parents had so far kept him patient by letting him drink all the soda and eat all the candy bars he wanted. "I haven't seen Aunt Louise in a whole year," said the little boy excitedly. "Do you think she brought me a present?"

"I'm sure she did, dear, Aunt Louise always brings the best presents. But don't ask Aunt Louise, because that would be rude. Wait until Aunt Louise gives it to you."

"Aunt Louise doesn't mind if I'm rude," said the little boy. "Aunt Louise likes me."

People close by hid smiles. They had either been an Aunt Louise themselves or had one.

Shirley Foyle phoned her parents. "The plane's late. Wouldn't you know? I'm a wreck."

"Now, honey. We told you we'd get Carly."

"I have to be the one. We have to start over again. I have to be here when she lands."

Shirl had done her hair for the occasion; as if Carly had ever cared how her sister's hair looked. Carly, who had been the type a year ago to shave her head and tattoo her skull.

"Chin up, darling," said her parents. "We'll see you both in a few hours."

Shirl hung up, savoring their voices. She pictured the homecoming. Carly and I, Shirl thought; we'll come in the front door, and Mom and Dad will—no; they'll be out on the lawn, yanking the taxi door open. They won't wait for us to come up the steps and cross the porch. Not when both their daughters are coming home together.

Carly. Coming home.

Shirl had not known how much she would miss her sister. The bathroom jostling, the giggles, the shared clothes, even the fights. Nobody could be as thoroughly satisfying or as thoroughly obnoxious as your only sister.

*My sister. Coming home.*

*Saturday: 7:09 P.M.*

Patrick had not looked at his watch in some time, but as he maneuvered another victim onto a backboard, and he and another man began the uphill struggle to carry the stretcher without tilting and terrifying the victim any more than he already was, somebody shouted out the time to somebody else.

The Golden Hour was up. Had been up for a long time.

He felt a queer chill around his eyes. It was not a physical sensation he had ever had before. It was as if his body said to him—*don't look, don't think, tune that out.*

It was like a horse wearing blinders: look straight ahead, keep working, keep believing you can save them. If you believe hard enough, you can make it work.

Patrick thought that maybe he knew what his mother meant: that the Golden Hour was similar to the Golden Rule. For in this grim night, he had seen only decency. He could not get over it, the way people were helping. It was almost as if they were glad to have the chance: as if the walking wounded were saying, So what if I'm a little bloody? I can still help. As if the neighbors were saying, So we had plans for Saturday night. So big deal. This is what matters.

We'll save them, he said to himself, very strongly.

And thought, in the corner of his mind that was calm and scientific, It's like clapping for Peter Pan to keep Tinker Bell alive. It's a fairy tale. These people we're taking out last—how can they make it? No matter how hard I clap, how can they make it?


*Saturday: 7:09:30* P.M.


From the hall phone came a voice full of wrath. "Where the hell is Life Star?"

Heidi had not heard much swearing. Now the absence of swearing struck her. The horror of the plane crash was beyond foolish four-letter words. Or perhaps swearing took energy, and nobody had any to spare.

So why was the fireman swearing?

He's helpless, thought Heidi. We've done all we can. Now we need something else. It isn't here, we can't get it, we can't make it happen, and he's afraid.

She had always thought of swearing as hostility. This was not. It was fear. It was like cold sweat.

"We've got the stretchers lined up!" yelled the fireman. "We've got the hospitals notified. We're Go. So where are the helicopters?"

She could not bear listening to the rising pitch of the fireman's voice, either; the tone that said, *People are dying and where are you?*

They're probably busy, thought Heidi. They didn't know a plane was coming down any more than I did. They're probably ferrying somebody else to a hospital. What are they supposed to do? Chuck him out and turn around?

A disaster is not just what happens, thought Heidi. It's also what comes next. Part of this is a second disaster.

She moved on, only to find herself next to Mr. Farquhar. He was yelling at some newly arrived volunteers. "Assume every single passenger has back injuries and internal injuries," he shouted angrily.

"Impact does that. Move nobody without proper support. You wanna kill 'em yourself? What's the matter with you?"

I moved eight people without ever thinking of that, Heidi thought. What if they die *because* I moved them? *What if I killed them?*

She swallowed a horrible-tasting swallow, like poison, hemlock, arsenic. But then, she had expected the rest of the plane to burn. She had thought speed mattered more than back support. Not that she had even known back support mattered at all.

These later rescue workers have more time than I did, she thought. I thought we had only a few seconds to work in. But the fire never went anywhere, and if there was more fuel, it's just sitting around in its tank.

Time.

A weird and perhaps meaningless thing. For the people in pain and terror, minutes were centuries passed in screaming. For the rescuers, the minutes were fractions—nothings—zeroes—in which they could hardly even get downhill, let alone move debris, slice through seat belts, get the backboard down, strap the patient on, and move him up the hill to where the medical teams could actually work.

There is no such thing as time, thought Heidi. Man invented it, but pain and fear are not acquainted with it.

It seemed to Heidi that the doctors on the scene were doing very little. She was rather angry at them. The ambulance volunteers were doing much more of the work.

I want to do this, thought Heidi. I want to do emergency work. I want to know what they know! I want to understand what they understand.

It occurred to Heidi that neither her brilliant father nor her successful mother would have had any idea what to do here, either. How they would have hated being helpless! They probably would have gone outdoors and directed traffic rather than submit to the sensation of not knowing what to do.

It came to her that it must take terrific courage for these volunteers: to walk right up to the unknown and start. She, Heidi, had been so demoralized by the unknown—like the piercing broken bone of the little girl Teddie—that she had fled. What courage it took not to flee. To do the best you could, however simple, and keep going. They are people who dare, thought Heidi. People who can take risk.

From somewhere had come large brightly colored cards with which each patient was tagged.

"Triage," explained the doctor.

Triage. Pronounced like tree: tree-ahj.

"French word," he said. "You divide the living into three groups. There are the ones who are going to be okay whether they get looked at quickly or not; we're putting them in the house, where it's warm and dry and they can take care of each other. They have a broken arm, or their forehead's split. It'll be too bad if they have a long wait, but none of them is going to die. Then we have the badly wounded. We divide those into the ones who are probably going to die no matter how much attention they get and the ones we can save if we get them help fast.

A hefty woman named Robyn was actually running triage.

On top of each patient's tag was writing space, and on the bottom were rip-off color strips. Robyn fastened tags to a button, a sleeve, a wrist. "Yellow," she said of one patient, ripping away the green strip and letting it fall to the ground.

"Red," she said for the next, ripping off both yellow and green.

"Black here," she told Heidi, who obediently ripped off green, yellow, and red, leaving that passenger with a tab and a black strip.

After a dozen taggings, Heidi understood.

A man who said his name was Gorp was sorting the patients like boxes for shipping: red guys here, yellow guys there.

"Why's he named Gorp?" Heidi asked Robyn.

"It's all he eats."

"What is?"

"Gorp." Robyn had better things to do than define nicknames, and she moved on.

Heidi was not clear. What was gorp? Some sort of fish? A European breakfast cereal?

Heidi and the doctor leaned against a wall, out of the way, sipping hot coffee. There was a whole group of people serving food from Heidi's kitchen. One of the patients whispered. "I'm thirsty, please; give me something to drink," but the doctor said no. "You're going into surgery as soon as we can get you there," he said. "Empty stomachs are better."

Heidi hated that. The poor man was wetting his dry lips with a dry tongue. Couldn't they do *something* for him? Maybe he could at least suck a Popsicle. Mrs. Camp had always been a great believer in the restorative power of Popsicles.

"We're waiting for the helicopters now," said the doctor, who had lost interest in the thirsty patient. "We've got a bunch we could airlift out. We have too many wounded for any one hospital to handle, and we're not particularly near any hospital anyway." The doctor looked pensive. "'Course, helicopters have a limited usefulness. Weather has to be right. Wind. Lots of times an ambulance is quicker." He frowned, and said to Heidi, "I could use another coffee, honey."

She took off to fetch it for him, thinking that she did not like that doctor much. He wasn't doing anything else, he could have gotten his own coffee. Going past Robyn she said, "Could the thirsty man at least have a sip of water?"

"Ice chips."

A woman of few words. Heidi liked that in a person. In the kitchen she flipped the exterior refrigerator door switch to CRUSH and stuck a cup under the opening. Instantly she had an inch of crushed ice for her man.

Mrs. Camp, wrapped in her robe, was giving orders, "Tuna fish," she was calling. "Frozen bread! Cans of soup! Get a move on. What are you people doing, anyway?"

The beautiful girl declined to get involved.

Heidi had learned her name. Darienne. The girl pronounced it leaning on the last syllable, making it rich and foreign. She had actually complimented Heidi on the furnishings and paintings of Dove House.

"Make sandwiches at least, Darienne," said Heidi sharply, leaving with her ice chips. "Everybody's been here a couple of hours and we have plenty to go."

The coffee shop, either being neighborly or being drafted, had come with every single food item they possessed at that hour on a Saturday night, mostly doughnuts and a whole lot of coleslaw. There weren't very many takers on the coleslaw. But they had several loaves of frozen bread, which Mrs. Camp was defrosting. There was not much left to make sandwich filling with now. Mrs. Camp tried to hand Darienne the peanut butter.

Darienne asked where the television was.

Heidi thought surely there was a plug somewhere to force Darienne's fingertips into, give her a much needed jolt. Here they thought the dog bite would whip Darienne into shape, but no, it had just put Darienne into a suing mode: Darienne sounded as if she were in court quite regularly, suing the entire world for getting in her way.

"Teenagers," said one passenger with loathing. He stared after Darienne as she walked toward the Gallery, looking left and right for a TV. "They're all like that. Teenagers today are disgusting. The most self-centered, worthless generation America has ever produced."

"And their music!" said another passenger. "These kids nauseate me."

Heidi was outraged. "I beg your pardon! What about me?" she demanded. "What about Patrick?"

"There are a few exceptions," the first passenger said, "but as a rule—"

"*Darienne*'s the exception!" yelled Heidi. She caught Mrs. Camp's eye on her, warning her to be courteous, and Heidi put the eye right back on Mrs. Camp. Mrs. Camp grinned. Heidi relaxed a little.

Heidi took her ice to her patient, but he had been moved. She found him in the front Gallery, in a yellow row, awaiting ambulance space. Beneath her father's prized artwork lay patients on stretchers, on thin ambulance blankets, and some right on the cold, hard, black-and-white marble. Kneeling beside her patient, Heidi, said, "Here are some ice chips to suck on. They might help a little."

He opened his mouth as if he were a baby expecting pureed peaches to be spooned in. Heidi shook a little ice onto his tongue. "Mm, mmm, good," said the man, grinning. It amazed her that everybody seemed to find something to grin about here.

She handed the cardiologist his coffee. He did not say thank you and he did not bother to look at her, either. She hated him now.

Ambulances in the courtyard inched up to the door. She kept her eyes on Robyn, who was making the triage decisions. What did Robyn see that told her which person to send next? What if Robyn was wrong? How could Robyn live with herself if she guessed wrong?

Mr. Farquhar squatted down beside her. "Come with me a moment?" he said.

She smiled at him. "Sure. I'm not doing anything right now. It's all sort of gotten beyond me. There are so many people here."

He nodded, but he wasn't listening. He was not a guidance counselor. Propping Heidi up was not on his list. When they were out of the Gallery and away from any patients, Mr. Farquhar said, "Heidi,

I need that big key ring you and Patrick had. We've got to open a different barn door."

She could not imagine why he had to take her away from the triage to say that. "Sure," she said. She frowned slightly. "But—the barn has no heat, Mr. Farquhar. You can't put people in there. I mean, it has been cleaned out since we stopped keeping horses, but still—it's not *clean*."

He looked at her without expression.

How specific did she have to be? Manure had lined those cement floors. Nobody with wounds could—

"For body bags," said Mr. Farquhar quietly. "Can't put them in the house with the survivors. They'll keep in the barn."

Like frozen meat, thought Heidi, and suddenly she was unbearably tired.

*Saturday: 7:14* P.M.

In the airport the families had begun pacing, had begun asking questions, had gotten cups of coffee-to-go at the little booth-style canteens at the end of the corridors, were flipping magazine pages without reading the words.

Shirl thought there really were an awful lot of airline personnel swarming around. People in those neat, attractive uniforms: the gentle, almost invisibly plaid wool; dark, charming silk at the throat: scarves, flowers, ascots, or regulation ties. Everybody was slim and neutral. Their faces were slim and neutral. Their voices were slim and neutral.

They formed almost a cordon around the waiting families and friends.

They seemed to be exchanging signals with their eyebrows.

She felt queerly surrounded. Like a fort.

Her hair knew something was wrong before she did. It prickled. Her scalp shivered.

The magazine pages stopped turning. The coffee cups were lowered. Talk dried up. One by one, the waiting group saw what Shirl saw.

There was something eerily un-American about it; as if they were going to be rounded up and deported for crimes they would never understand.

A pleasant-looking woman with gray hair spoke into the microphone at the ticket desk. Shirl's heart began beating arrythmically. She had strange cramps in the backs of her legs.

Sitting too long, Shirl told herself casually. Need to get up and walk around.

In a slow, uninformative voice, the woman divided her speech into easily grasped short segments. "I'm going to ask everyone . . . waiting for flight One One Six . . . to follow us . . . to the banquet room at the airport hotel. . . . It's a short walk . . . down the corridor . . . and to the right. . . . Airline staff . . . will lead the way."

Airline staff were already gently prodding, corralling people, using fingertips on shoulders and palms on the center of backs.

In gasping, fish-dead silence, people took the first few steps forward.

Shirl had difficulty standing.

A heavyset man holding a balloon bouquet stumbled next to her. Shirl took his arm. He gripped hers tightly. But he didn't seem to see her. His collection of silver and cartooned balloons bobbed in front of them.

Shirl closed off her mind. She would ask no questions. She would not say the terrible words.

It was out of the question.

It could not happen.

Not to your own sister.

No.

The plane had been rerouted. Yes. Snowstorms. It had landed in Canada, perhaps. Or Baltimore. Yes.

Yes, it was nothing.

Nothing at all.


*Saturday: 7:30* P.M.

Outside Dove House came the volcanic explosion of rotors.

Life Star was here. What a fabulous name! It gave life; it shone of stars and eternal skies. Another Christmas word.

The helicopter had landed a good half mile away, in the farthest possible corner of the pony field. The "pad" was illuminated, but with what light Heidi could not imagine. Even the Invader Lights didn't glow that far.

She ran to the back porch, where in summer, white wicker rockers with pretty plump cushions sat in a long leisurely row. There she watched the first stretcher being toted through the wreckage, across the fields, over a stream. She knew that stream. Deep enough to soak every boot that went in it. She shivered for them.

Rescuers' fingers were numb. Bulky layers of clothing were soaked. Everybody had fallen several times. Kneecaps and ankles were bruised and tired.

As they neared the helicopter, the stretcher bearers ducked down, and even at this distance, Heidi could see the rotors flinging wet wind into their faces. And then she could see something else. Where she had pictured a hospital under the rotor—space for dozens—Life Star had room for two stretchers.

*Two.*

No more than the ambulances!

What was this nonsense of taking two at a time? We'll be here forever, Heidi thought. Two by two, like animals in the Ark. We don't have time to save the world two by two.

But I'm not saving anybody at all, she thought. I'm just standing on the porch, gawking, while other people do the work.

She went back in, went up to Robyn for work, and Robyn without comment handed Heidi an IV bag to hold aloft so it would drip into the vein of a passenger. Heidi looked into the patient's eyes. It was a girl about her own age. "Hi," said Heidi inadequately. "How are you?"

Both she and the patient giggled nervously.

"Pretty good," said the girl. Her speech was slurred. It sounded like, *Pree guh.* "I thought I was a goner for a while," she added. It sounded like, *Thaw wuzza . . . goner . . . frile.* There was something terrifying about the words, as if a person whose lips could not move would soon have a heart that did not move.

The girl's tag was red. It had a tiny symbol: a rabbit running. It meant—hurry up! Move this one next!

Quick like a bunny, thought Heidi. She had had a nanny once who used to say that all the time, when Heidi was getting dressed, when Heidi was getting in the car, when Heidi was eating a snack. Quick like a bunny.

But there were too many people with red tags for everybody to be taken quick like a bunny.

"I'm Heidi," said Heidi.

The girl's color was dreadful. It almost seemed lavender; a pastel shade, not a color human beings of any race normally came in.

"Carly," whispered the girl. She smiled. With a great effort she said clearly, because it was so important, "I'm on my way home."

"That's great," said Heidi. She had never felt so inadequate. Robyn paused next to Carly's stretcher. An ambulance must have arrived. Robyn was choosing the two patients to go on it. Heidi was sure they would take Carly next. Anybody could see that Carly was in desperate shape.

But Robyn shook her head fractionally to the attendants and passed Carly by. Two other patients were lifted onto stretchers. Both were also reds. And they, quick like a bunny, were hospital bound. But it's been a long time, thought Heidi. It's been more than an hour and a half. That's not quick like a bunny.

The girl's hand was cold, but so was Heidi's. "Do you want another blanket?" said Heidi. "Carly?"

Carly murmured something. Her lips curved slightly. Almost a smile. Heidi said, "Carly, I'm here."

"My sister," said Carly.

"I'll talk to your sister."

"Tell her," said Carly.

"I'll tell her," said Heidi.

Carly smiled.

Tell the sister what? thought Heidi. What is her name? What do I say? Tears shaped like big puddles, thick pudding-y tears, filled Heidi's eyes and spread over her face. Carly didn't see. She and her soft smile were somewhere else. "Hang on, Carly," said Heidi over and over. "Hang on. You can make it."


*Saturday: 7:55 P.M.*


Daniel had been telling Mrs. Jemmison about his family for an hour. He knew because she told him the time whenever he asked. He also knew by now that she did not know about Tuck; she had just said that to be kind. "It wasn't kind," said Daniel. "I want to know."

Mrs. Jemmison asked somebody else to go up and find a thirteen-year-old boy and see if he was hurt and if so, how much. Daniel knew they would not tell him the truth, if it was really bad.

"Your mom and dad sound like great people," said Mrs. Jemmison. "'Course I know we'll be in touch, them and me, talking about this. I'll be your number-one visitor in the hospital, Daniel. Your mom and dad, we'll have them over for dinner."

I forgot Mom and Dad are divorced, thought Daniel. I forgot about Linda and the wedding.

Around him the Jaws ripped metal away. People finally being moved from their crushed agony screamed in new agony. People swore, and stumbled, and cursed the weather and the cold and the ice.

Daniel thought, She asked about my family and I told her. Because they still are my family, no matter how many Lindas and weddings there are.

He thought, But I don't have time to tell Dad that now. I don't have time to tell him I'm sorry about all the things I said to him. I'm going to die.

"Mrs. Jemmison?" he said. His voice was going to go on him. He could feel his throat starting to thicken and his chin get weak. "Would you tell my mom and dad something for me?" He willed himself not to get all sentimental and mushy while he gave her the message. He said, "Tell Dad it's okay about Linda. Tell him I love him. Tell Mom—" he knew what Mom would want to know. That she had raised a good kid; that he loved her and would do his best.

My best isn't much now, Mom, he thought. Just breathing. That's my max. He said. "Tell Mom she did good. I'm all right."

He knew that Mrs. Jemmison knew what he was saying; not that his body was all right; not that he was surviving the plane crash all right; but that his life had been all right.

# Ten

After they finished the run, Laura's crew cleaned the ambulance while the driver headed back to Dove House. They had to stop for gas because the dispatcher said that the local hospital was already overloaded; their next run would be all the way to Hartford Hospital. The first time she went out on the ambulance, Laura had been amazed to find out the first thing you did coming back to the barn was put gas in the tank. Somehow you didn't think of ambulances like that; they just came; you didn't think of maintenance.

But, in fact, as much time was spent cleaning, restocking, checking lists, and double checking gas, oil, windshield-wiper fluid, and so forth, as was spent actually transporting patients.

This time they carried the two stretchers into Dove House, where Robyn, a hundred-years-ago girlfriend of Laura's father, was running triage. Laura stepped into Dove House and thought it was the most beautiful place she had ever seen in her life. The marble gleamed, the paintings looked like those in rich museums, and the stairs were meant for Cinderella. Laura could not even imagine what it must be like to be Heidi Landseth and live there all the time.

Robyn directed them to take a woman who had been virtually stapled to the ground by a long metal rod. She had been carried up to the house with the rod still in her, the wound sealed front and back, and her body propped at a tilt with rolled blankets. Laura could not imagine why the woman, whose entire body was lacerated, was not dead. Robyn obviously felt the patient had a solid chance. A plastic tube had been inserted into the patient's nose and down into her throat to keep her airway clear, and an oxygen mask, like a little see-through pyramid, rested over the opening.

The patient's teeth were chattering and she was shivering uncontrollably. Laura recognized the jacket that was tucked around her: it was a Nearing River High School team jacket. She took it off gently and replaced it with a cotton thermal blanket. The jacket back read FARQUHAR.

Patrick had wrapped this woman in his jacket.

He must be frozen by now, thought Laura. She hoped Patrick would see her, would know they were on the same team at the same hour, that he had trained Laura well, and with any luck develop a crush on Laura.

It was not the kind of house with a peg on the wall to toss a dirty jacket on. She threw it to Robyn instead, and then she and her crew mate carried the patient out of the beautiful hallway and into the windy, smoke-stinking chill of the courtyard.

Laura locked the stretcher in place in the ambulance and held the woman's wrist gently between her fingers to take a pulse. A bracelet fell back against Laura's long, manicured nails. It was a charm bracelet, with silhouettes of children. Four children, Laura could not help tilting each charm and reading the names and birth dates. This was the mother of Sarah, Matthew, Joshua, and Stephanie. The oldest was fifteen.

Tears blinded Laura.

For a moment she was utterly useless.

She wiped the tears away fiercely with the back of her wrist and gritted her teeth. She would not cry. She would do her job. She would do what she could.

Laura's family was, as her father put it, "very lapsed" Roman Catholic. She had been to Mass no more than a half dozen times in her seventeen years. She had been a spectator at somebody else's sport. Now, as she wrote down the pulse—it wasn't strong—and took the blood pressure—it wasn't good—Laura prayed for the first time in her life. *Jesus, Mary, and Joseph,* prayed Laura. *Let her be okay.*

*Saturday: 7:59 P.M.*

There is, thought Heidi, an element of Opening Night to this show. We all went to separate dress rehearsals. We all know a little bit of the script, but not quite enough to get it all together. Because it's a disaster. That's what a disaster is, I guess. When something is too wrong to make it all right. When you can do your very best, hundreds of you, and still fall short.

"Grab this side!" said a fireman suddenly, loudly.

Heidi jumped up from Carly's side and caught one end of a stretcher. The patient on it had not been strapped down right and had started falling off. Heidi went out to the ambulance to be sure nothing else happened.

She was completely unprepared for the scene in the courtyard.

TV people had arrived, and their amazingly brilliant lights were being used to illuminate the scene. They were busily interviewing and filming and peering into vehicles and faces. They offended her. How dare they? People were in pain, they were afraid, they were bloody, their clothes were torn—and they were photographed without permission anyway.

She almost stormed over and ordered them off her property.

And yet, in some way, it was not her property.

It was a plane crash; it was everybody's property.

As the ambulance doors slammed and the vehicle pulled off, Heidi heard a televeision reporter speaking into a microphone. "The Dove House Crash is the worst in recent memory," said the woman, in that strong carrying voice people got when they had an audience.

The Dove House Crash, thought Heidi.

No. Please. Don't name this after my house! I don't want to be in magazines and histories like that. The Sioux City crash, the Avianca crash, the Lockerbie, Scotland, crash . . . The Dove House Crash.

She had looked so intensely at the reporter that the woman turned, saw Heidi, and took a step closer. Heidi fled. The last thing she wanted to do was be filmed when she looked like this. The thought of how she must look made Heidi ill. She headed back to Carly's side again, only to be stopped at her very own front door.

"Sorry, miss," said a policeman firmly. "We're not letting anybody in."

"I live here," said Heidi.

"Right," he said sarcastically.

She probably looked like a dead mouse. They would probably interview Darienne, thinking Darienne lived here. They'd probably let Darienne come and go like the Queen of England. She said, "Really, I'm Heidi Landseth; it's my house."

"Do you have identification?" he said. He actually said that. Heidi could have slugged him.

"It is her house, Dave," said the fireman HARRIS, the first uniformed personnel she'd met on the scene.

They all laughed. Heidi's was forced.

"Nice of you to drop in," said Dave, apologizing.

"Why aren't you letting people in the house, though?" she said.

He smiled sadly. "World is full of weirdos. People who want to gawk, people who want to help but will just be in the way, people who want to do a little looting while the doors are open."


*Saturday:* 8:05 P.M.


Patrick reached down to help tighten the stretcher straps.

"I'll do that," said the burly man shouldering Patrick out of the way. Patrick was too big to shoulder away, and he glared at the man.

"It's nice of you young people to try to help," said the man, "but now that trained personnel are on the scene, the best thing for you to do is stay out of the way."

I'll deck him, thought Patrick. I'll redivide his ribs. I'll—

"You heard the man," the paramedic said sharply to Patrick. "This is not a game, kid. This is life and death. Now get out of the way."

Patrick said, "I'm fully trained. I'm an EMT. Have been for two years. I had a hundred and ninety hours of—"

The men paid no attention to him.

The patient said, "He's only a *boy?* I thought he was older. Thank goodness you men are here."

Patrick wanted to kick right through the stretcher. It took a real effort to remember that this was not good patient/rescuer protocol. He held his breath, tightened his jaw, and backed away. He had to look down at his hands to order the fists to uncurl.

He found his father. "Dad, they're trying to kick me out."

"Who?"

"Adults."

His father simply nodded. "You'll have to accept it."

"*What?* Dad!"

"Patrick, they do have more experience, they do have more training, you are younger. No escaping those facts. This is not the time or the place to discuss it. Plenty of work to do that doesn't involve wounded."

His own father. Patrick couldn't believe it. It was years since he had had a screaming match with his own father. In fact, he vividly remembered the last swear-slinging. Patrick had gotten into a fight with the ref at a soccer game, when Patrick was called out sides and he wasn't. His father'd dragged him off the field, practically strangling Patrick by his T-shirt, saying, "Whether he's right or wrong doesn't count, son, he's the referee. Shut your mouth."

Patrick had not shut his mouth. Patrick had hauled out every word he knew to arouse adult rage. Patrick had also been grounded for the rest of the soccer season, by both parent and coach.

The words came back to him and the urge to scream at the top of his lungs was so strong he actually put the back of his hand against his lips to cut it off.

His father didn't even notice, just strode off. *He* had things to do. Whereas Patrick, his own son, his own flesh and blood, had been kicked off the team. And his father wasn't going to do a thing about it.

Heidi said, "I know how you feel. I just got refused entry to my own house."

"They can't do that," said Patrick, slamming his right fist into his left palm.

"Well, they did," said Heidi, folding her arms with such ferocity she might have been carving meat.

They glared fiercely at the world, and since the world was much too busy, they glared at each other. Heidi was suddenly aware of her protruding sulky lower lip, her grinding jaw, her frown-lined forehead. She exploded into laughter. Patrick laughed later, and less, but at least he laughed. He said, "I hate being a kid. All my life I've hated being a kid. It's such a worthless thing to be."

Heidi understood but didn't agree. "I like being a kid," she said. "But the thing is, you get sick of it before the adults do. They want you to be a child until you're out of college. I'm ready to quit now."

"How old are you?" asked Patrick.

"Sixteen. I'm a sophomore. I've seen you in school."

"I'm eighteen in two months. I'm a senior. I live for graduation."

She smiled at him, counting off the time. "March, April, May, June. I guess you can live that long."

He grinned for real this time, nodding. "What day is your birthday?"

"May tenth."

"Hey, how about that! Mine's May eleventh. Let's celebrate together. What do you want for your birthday? I could give you a plane piece."

"Sick-o," she said. "Anyway, they're mine and I'll probably be picking them out of my woods for years to come."

"Perfume? Scarf? Twisted, perverted videos?"

"Actually," said Heidi, "for my birthday you could sign me up to learn what you learned."

"Lady, nobody will ever learn as much as I've learned."

She laughed. "Uh-huh. I mean rescue. I want to know what you know."

"No adult thinks I know anything," said Patrick gloomily.

"They will in June, so shut up. Whereas I really don't know anything. How do I learn?"

"They run teaching sessions twice a year. You can take the summer one." He smiled. "I'll probably be the instructor," he said. "I mean, who else will have had plane-crash experience?"

"Me," she pointed out. "Next time a plane crashes on my land, I'm going to be able to take control and save lives and stop bleeding and back up transport vehicles."

"So there," said Patrick, laughing.

"Better believe it," said Heidi.


*Saturday: 8:12 P.M.*


Daniel had a mission now. He could not move; the pain was so great that sometimes he could not really even think, but he had resolved to die bravely. He thought of brave deaths, like Davy Crockett at the Alamo, soldiers at Gettysburg, soldiers in Vietnam or on the beaches on D-Day, and he said to himself, They toughed it out. I'll tough it out.

Mrs. Jemmison had managed to get a tiny bit of chocolate bar up to him, and it was melting in his mouth. It was wonderful, he loved it, he wanted to write a hundred letters to the chocolate bar company and tell them they had saved his life.

That made him smile a little. Nothing was going to save his life.

"I'm right here," said Mrs. Jemmison, "I'm just shifting position a little bit."

But when she moved, he could see a different angle out of the corner of his eye, and he realized that somebody was helping her put on special gear; fire gear; she was getting into big yellow pants, strapping on a breathing pack, getting ready to lower the big plastic gas mask over her face.

Nobody said anything.

They didn't want to scare him. He could tell that there was pointing and miming going on.

"Mrs. Jemmison?" said Daniel.

"I'm here, honey. We're not going anywhere."

So there was fire.

"Is the fire starting? Is it near me?" He didn't feel any heat. He couldn't hear any crackling or smell actual smoke. He knew the fuel smell was still there, but he had gotten used to it by now.

She said, "It's not near you, honey."

So there was fire.

She said, "You were telling me about your family."

He said, "Do you have a gun?"

"No, honey. Why?"

"If you have to leave me here when it burns, will you shoot me first? I don't want to feel it burning me."

# Eleven

"We've got eighteen walking wounded I'd like to see at the hospital," said the fire chief. His voice crackled on the radio. Ty listened sullenly. The only reason anybody at all had gotten to any hospital at all was because he, Ty, had cleared the road. And was he getting thanks? No. He wasn't even getting a replacement. The only thrill left in his life was listening to the talk of people actually having a thrill.

He considered the best way to get even with Laura. It should involve pain and last a long time.

"We could move 'em in a school bus," said the unknown voice the fire chief was talking to. "We got enough EMT's to take care of 'em. Practically the whole state responded. Might as well give 'em a job."

The fire chief said, "So where's a school bus at?"

Ty jumped into the frequency. "I can get the bus up here!" He omitted to mention that he had never driven a bus in his life. He said, "I know where they are." He omitted to mention that the ten-foot wire corral in which the school buses were kept was locked against vandalism. He definitely did not mention that he, Ty, could pick the lock and had once, in his junior-high years, keyed a school bus to demonstrate his hatred of school in general. He hadn't been caught, which was one of Ty's mottoes in life.

"Who's this?" said the fire chief.

"Ty Maronn."

"Get it," said the fire chief.

In the dark road, Ty leapt into the air, failed to click his heels, but did at least land upright. He whirled, his grin burgeoning to encompass his entire body: even his chest, expanding as he ran, felt friendlier toward the world. Maybe he would let Laura live after all.

Ty raced back to his parked truck, planning his bus theft. Which school bus should he take, the good new one with automatic or that old one with hard seats but the best heater?

At last, at last, he had something to do.

"Hey!" shouted the policeman.

Heidi and Patrick looked at him from across the courtyard.

"Me?" said Heidi, eyebrows lifted to question, finger pointing to her own chest.

"You!"

"They're probably going to accuse you of looting," said Patrick. "You'd probably better not even go to your room and brush your hair."

They grinned at each other and jogged over to the policeman.

"Can you round up your dogs?" said the policeman plaintively. "They are all over the house. Especially the little ones. The little yippy ones make me want to—uh—" he quit talking, pasting a fake smile on his face.

"Me, too," Heidi said. "They're not my dogs, anyway; they're my mother's. She has great taste in everything but dogs."

Once again she was bounding all over Dove House trying to scoop up Winnie and Clemmie, while yelling "Down, Fang!" It was so humiliating. And now that she thought about it, so was Patrick's remark about brushing her hair. At the time she thought it was a good joke; now she wondered if he was trying, oh so subtly, to let her know she needed to look in a mirror.

Patrick, however, did not strike Heidi as a particularly subtle person.

She had just caught Winnie and was heading for Mrs. Camp's room to put the dog in for the last time, maybe even tape the door shut, when she saw, in the library, leaning against the elegant marble fireplace, her hair reflecting the civilized little fire somebody had actually started in there, Darienne. Looking beautiful, looking sweet, looking perfect, looking into a TV camera lens.

Heidi's mouth fell open.

They were interviewing the one teenager who really *was* scum? They were interviewing the one person out of all the hundreds on Dove House land who was *not* helping?

Heidi even recognized the interviewer. One of her favorite anchors. Not just some old reporter. An anchor. Somebody Heidi would have been thrilled to meet. Thrilled even to see across a room.

In my library! thought Heidi. Interviewing Darienne!

Clemmie wandered innocently by, and Heidi caught the second dog, tucked one under each arm, and headed for the library. She seemed to be holding fringed pillows. The pillows croaked. She really was holding them a bit too tightly.

"Oh, Darienne?" said Heidi.


*Saturday: 8:20 P.M.—*
*Nearing River, Connecticut*
*5:20 P.M.—San Diego, California*
*Sunday 2:20 A.M.—Geneva, Switzerland*

Alex Landseth struggled to find the ringing telephone in his unfamiliar hotel room. When he finally had it in hand, he could not remember what country he was in, nor what language to respond in. "Hello," he muttered, blinking, trying to focus on the little glowing digital alarm clock he kept by his bed.

"Alex!" said his wife urgently. Alex tried to remember where Rebecca was right now. Nothing came to mind. But the sound of the phone—the distant, whistling emptiness—told Alex Landseth it was a world away. "Whassa matter?" he said.

"There's been a plane crash."

His mind cleared instantly. It wasn't Rebecca who'd crashed: she was talking. It wasn't Heidi: Heidi hadn't been going anywhere. So it was somebody who mattered enough for a middle-of-the-night call, but not the two most important people in Alex's world. "Who?" he said, sitting up, already afraid, already shivering.

"Not *who. Where.* Our house, Alex! The plane came down in our yard, on top of the rose garden. I just saw a news flash. They're calling it the Dove House Crash."

"Oh my god, Becca! Is Heidi all right? Did it hit the house? Is she hurt? Did you call?"

"I don't know. I couldn't get through. The phone's busy. I tried the Steins and the Kelleys, and nobody answered." The Steins and the Kelleys were the only people in Nearing River they really knew.

Alex Landseth tried to quiet his leaping heart. "Mrs. Camp is there," he said. "She'll know what to do."

The unspoken statement between them was that Heidi would not know what to do. Heidi mystified and depressed them. She had not turned out to be the daughter they had expected. She was not outstanding at anything. They kept telling themselves she was a late bloomer; she would find herself in a few years; she would develop enthusiasms and talents as a sophomore . . . well, then, a junior . . . a senior . . . in college, maybe . . .

"Okay, let's think," said Rebecca Landseth. "Who else can I call?"

"The rector at St. Anne's?" said Alex. The family went to church three times a year: Christmas Eve, Easter Sunday, and Mother's Day. Plus they contributed the holly to decorate the churches for Advent.

"Good idea. He can find out if Heidi's all right."

Alex felt nauseated and ice cold. He huddled under the duvet and wished he were home on their heated waterbed. "They'll have an information phone line started pretty soon," said Alex. "They always do for things like this. Keep the TV on, and the minute they put the 800 number up, call. Now, what did the TV show? The house? The plane?"

"The plane's a 747," she began.

"Of course," said Alex Landseth. It couldn't be some ordinary old plane. It had to be the biggest. And he couldn't be staying tonight in a Hilton, where he'd have a television and with cable be able to pick up US Army stations; no, he had opted for European ambiance and there was no TV in the entire hotel.

"It's broken up pretty badly. One wing was separated and caught fire, but it seemed to be downhill from the house, maybe in the pony field. It was hard to tell from the angle of the camera. The camera filmed—conservatively speaking—a thousand trucks in the court-yard, and they were carrying wounded out our front door. So I don't think there's too much damage to the house," said Rebecca.

Alex thought that if one wing had been flung into the pony field, the other could easily have been flung into his study. He loved the house. Only Heidi loved it more. And Burke was not there. He had National Guard this weekend. Alex could not imagine how Heidi and Mrs. Camp would cope with this. They were people who pre-ferred very narrow boundaries: groceries and TV choices were about Mrs. Camp's limit, while catching the school bus and taking the dogs out seemed to be Heidi's.

"Maybe Burke'll bring his unit down," said Alex, trying to joke, picturing his beloved daughter, who rarely got anything right, who was so easily humiliated and stumped.

Alex and Rebecca Landseth were helpless.

It was not a situation in which they had ever found themselves.

More than anything they were angry; angry that they could not phone home, take charge, be sure, check, or know.

Alex sat through the night, watching the little red numbers on his clock slowly changing, waiting for his wife to ring again.

Rebecca sat stabbing the button on her phone, telephoning everybody she could think of, and finally calling the Connecticut State Police, who said they had plenty of people on the scene, and as far as they knew, nobody from the house was hurt.

"But you don't know for sure," said Rebecca Landseth.

"No, ma'am. We'll check. Stay by your phone. We'll get back to you as soon as we can."

Rebecca knew by the tone of voice that it wouldn't be any time soon; it was not their top priority. She told herself that this was reasonable; top priorities had to be saving the injured and preventing the spread of fire; but she was a parent, and a scared parent cannot be reasonable. She screamed at the state policeman until she was hoarse, and the state policeman said implacably, "Yes, ma'am. We're going to check, ma'am. Stay by your phone. We'll get back as soon as we can."

*Saturday: 8:31 P.M.*

Heidi was almost inside the door of the library when Darienne pirouetted, her mouth making a little smile of sophistication and pride. Ugh, thought Heidi. Darienne's complexion, in the firelight and the spotlight, was incredibly lovely. She had been designed for things like this.

*Complexion*. thought Heidi.

*Skin color.*

*Carly!* I left her alone. I was holding her hand, and I got up to do something—do what?—it couldn't have been important—but whatever it was, I left her there. Alone.

Heidi forgot Darienne. Darienne was nothing, had been proving that all night. Heidi rushed down the Gallery, checking patients. Looking for Carly. The dogs yipped on. This was a breed with an incredible capacity for making noise. She didn't see Carly, could not believe she still had the dogs to deal with, raced upstairs, put the ankle biters in Mrs. Camp's room for the last time, and rushed back down.

A more careful check this time. Still no Carly. What a relief. They had finally put Carly in an ambulance.

She sighed. She did not need to worry about Carly now. Other people had worried for her.

The entire evening was so amazing. The kindness of strangers was such an incredibly beautiful thing. Yet another Christmas analogy came to her: some irritated innkeeper having to deal with some woman dumb enough to give birth on the road. But he was kind to strangers. All these people: they were all strangers: to the passengers, to each other, to Heidi, to Dove House, some of them even strangers to Connecticut. Two New York State ambulances had arrived, and helicopters out of Springfield, Massachusetts.

And all these strangers, with all their kindness and skill, were not getting on TV.

Darienne was getting on TV.

It was enough to make you want to strap the girl to a stretcher of nails and tape her mouth to her hair.

Heidi was headed back to the library to stop Darienne when she saw an old afghan on the couch in the Hall, twitching. How could Clemmie or Winnie possibly have gotten down there? Heidi was furious. She strode into the Hall. Mrs. Camp was capable of making truly ugly crochet: her favorite colors were mud brown, avocado green, and turquoise blue. Maybe it's Tally, thought Heidi hopefully, although he was too big to hide under the afghan. She tweaked it aside, and there, beneath, lay the very first passenger Heidi had failed to rescue.

Teddie.

It seemed years ago. How could this child still be in the house? Heidi knelt down beside the little girl. "Hey, Teddie," she said.

Teddie's face seemed greasy. She had a sickly glint to her skin. How long had she been lying here? thought Heidi, horrified.

"The man said he would call," said Teddie. Her voice quavered. "But he didn't."

Had Teddie fallen asleep—or lost consciousness—and been forgotten in the confusion? Was she so small that they had not remembered her? Mrs. Camp had set Teddie on the couch—but all the other wounded had been laid carefully on the floor, as flat as possible, and tagged. Teddie was not tagged.

"I started with a quarter," said Teddie, holding up a palm with dangling Mickey Mouse Band-Aids. "I lost my quarter when we crashed. The tapes came off. And the man didn't phone Mommy and

Daddy. They don't know I'm here. They won't be able to find me. And now I can't call."

"That's okay. We'll find them. They'll come."

Teddie shook her head. She had heard this line before.

Heidi thought, What's the matter with me? "Be right back, Teddie." Heidi ran into the kitchen, where she and Burke and Mrs. Camp dumped their change into an immense restaurant-sized jar that had once held about a million portions of peanut butter. They played a lot of card games for small change and were always betting on televised sports. The pot got all. Someday they were going to take a fabulous vacation on the money, but they hadn't gotten around to planning the details yet. Shoveling down among the pennies. Heidi rooted around until she came up with a quarter. Then she got some adhesive tape from Robyn and went back to Teddie. "Here," she said. "One phone-call quarter."

Teddie smiled up at her. What an adorable smile!

Heidi carefully taped the quarter down, winding the tape between Teddie's small fingers to be sure that this time, it stuck.

How awful to be little, thought Heidi, and not understand. Not know that if she couldn't find Mommy, Mommy would find her; not know that all these strangers would take care of her.

Teddie's body seemed slack. Her tears seemed to dry up, as if nothing existed anymore to provide them. Her eyes stayed open. They did not blink. "Teddie?" whispered Heidi. She pulled back from the little body. She found her own lungs impossible to fill; her breathing had become a hundred tiny spasms. She ran to find a doctor.

But with all the people filling her house, her yard and field and barn, she seemed to be alone. For one horrifying twilight-zoned minute, she and Teddie were the only people on earth, the only people in Dove House.

The others were moving patients to Life Star or to ambulances. They were going out the back and front, loaded down. She would make them take Teddie next; they had to take Teddie next; she would insist on it. It was her house, wasn't it? The helicopter was landing on her grass, right?

Heidi grabbed the shoulder of the only person she recognized, the man Gorp. "There's a little girl inside, I don't like how she looks, nobody has checked her at all, she looks as if—"

"In a minute," said Gorp. "You stay with her until I get there."

I left Teddie alone a second time, thought Heidi. Just like Carly. Am I afraid of being next to them in case they die? Do I run away and pretend to be getting help, when really I'm just a coward? How am I going to telephone Teddie's mother and father? Do I say, Well, I was busy, and I had other things to do, so Teddie died alone.

She saw Patrick.

"Patrick," she said, grabbing him, hauling him with her.

"What?"

"The little girl, the first one, Teddie, I think she's dying."

He went with her.

"In shock," said Patrick briefly. He and Heidi slid a backboard under Teddie, and Patrick elevated the entire board with books off a shelf in the Hall, getting Teddie's feet above her head. By now Heidi knew the shock trousers, which were pumped up to keep the blood in the head and heart, couldn't be pulled over the broken bone. "Robyn!" he called. "Oxygen here."

Robyn was with him in a moment, little muscles around her jaw clenching and unclenching. "Children do this," she said.

Heidi raised her eyebrows to ask what children did.

"Mask shock very well," said Robyn. She lubricated and slid in an airway, which would have made Heidi scream and gag, but Teddie put up no resistance. Robyn said comfortingly, "Now, it'll be easier to breathe, sweetie pie, much much easier. You just hold old Patrick's hand here, and you know what? We're going to take you for a helicopter ride!" She attached oxygen. "Won't that be neat? Boy, will you have stories to tell Mommy and Daddy now!"

She said aside to Heidi, "And then they crash, just like that."

The word *crash* hit Heidi like a slap. Was Robyn saying the helicopter was going to crash?

"She means going into shock," whispered Patrick quickly. "Crash. Like sleeping a long time after you stay up studying? Crash?"

Don't crash, Teddie, she prayed.

She felt a queer buzzing in her own head; the same airless rata-tat-tat that had drilled her thoughts when this whole nightmare began; one that somehow removed Heidi from what was really happening.

"Patrick?" she said dimly.

"Yeah?" He was taking Teddie's vital signs again, writing them down on a card, tying it to Teddie's jacket.

"I'm losing it," Heidi said.

He smiled at her. It was a tired, gentle smile. An old man's smile. She was so touched, she wanted to stroke his face and coax the lips to turn up more. He took Heidi's hand in his and transferred Teddie's little hand into Heidi's. "You'll be fine," he said to them both.

Robyn said, "Okay, guys, let's get another blanket over Teddie and get her on down the hill to Life Star." She said, "Teddie, honeybunch, you'll be able to breathe just fine, and Heidi here is going to hang onto your hand. Why, before you know it, you're going to be all warm and cozy in a nice hospital bed! You be my good girl now, okay?"

Teddie, unable to speak, nodded under the plastic mask. But her blue lips closed and her little cheeks sagged.

Heidi was displaced; helicopter personnel took Teddie's stretcher, men who clucked like sets of grandmothers, stroking and soothing.

Heidi was somewhat irritated that the majority of the rescuers were men. Heidi had never had a feminist thought in her life. It was totally not interesting to her whether a man did something or a woman did. Now she cared. For every Robyn working, there were ten Mr. Farquhars. Heidi wanted more women out there saving lives instead of making coffee.

She pictured her few girl friends. She could not imagine Karen or Jacqueline planning to serve the sick and the wounded instead of spending the day at the mall. Or would they, too, have risen to the occasion? Done their very best? Been their very kindest?

"Give me a hand," said Gorp to her, and she ripped open an envelope of bandages for him.

She had not dared ask questions before; the pace was too desperate; but now everything had slowed. She pointed to Gorp's hands. Although he was outdoors as much as in, he was not wearing winter gloves but thin disposable white surgical gloves. Almost all the real rescue workers—the ones in uniforms; the trained ones—were also wearing disposable gloves.

"Why?" she asked Gorp.

"AIDS."

She stared at him. "At a plane crash?"

He laughed without humor. "Who knows who's on board?" he said. "It's fine to rescue people, but it's not so fine to contract a fatal disease while you're doing it. Gloving is protocol for every rescue group in the state. Lots of squads require double gloving."

She stared down at her hands, the bare hands that had briefly held Carly's and Teddie's and so many others.

Gloving is protocol, she repeated in her head.

Other people's jargon took time to be understood.

The three words zinged around in her already rata-tat-tatting head, and somehow as she considered it, the "g" fell off, until the words that thrummed for Heidi were, Loving is protocol.


*Saturday: 8:42 P.M.*

Tuck MacArthur would worship Ty Maronn the rest of his life.

When the school bus pulled up into the courtyard, and the eighteen walking wounded climbed on, Tuck looked around longingly. "I've never driven anything in my life," said Tuck sadly. "I'm thirteen, and my father was going to let me start driving, but they got divorced, and I live with my mother, and she's a scaredy-cat about everything and probably won't let me drive until I'm ninety."

Ty knew how serious this was. He had a mother like that, too, but luckily his parents had not divorced, and his father had sneaked him out real young. They used to go out at dawn to practice driving when his dad said the laws didn't count because nobody else was on the road. Ty had a lot more years of driving experience than anybody his age was legally allowed to have.

Ty pulled the skinny little kid toward him so a passenger considerably more wounded could get on the bus. "Keep your voice down, kid," said Ty. He figured this Tuck was the type who probably snitched forbidden chocolate and forgot to wash his mouth off afterward. "You be good," said Ty, "and when we get on the straightaway, I'll let you drive."

Tuck's mouth sagged. He stared at Ty in awe. In love. "Let me drive?" he repeated.

"Shh," said Ty.

The bus filled.

The walking wounded were by now much more bored than they were hurt. They had helped a great deal during the first hour, assisting others up to the house, and so forth, but then what seemed like several hundred disaster-trained volunteers appeared on the scene, and the walking-wounded set was retired to the back of the house. It was like being in jail. They got reprimanded whenever they tried to escape. Their keepers brought them food—odd food, like coleslaw; these people were really peddling coleslaw—but basically, when they left their room, they were in the way and got sent back.

Tuck had been sent flying through the air when his seat ripped loose, but his only real wound was a split lip. He and two others went the wrong way trying to reach safety from the fire and spent some time in the woods. They finally circled the flaming wing, way off through a bumpy stumpy field, and one of the survivors got hung up on some old barbed wire, so they had to peel him loose from that, in the dark, and they all fell into another little stream, of which the property seemed to have dozens, and when they finally reached the house on the hill, they were frozen stiff and got sent up to a bathroom to rest their feet in warm tub water.

Tuck had asked everybody about his brother, but when he said they'd been sitting near the wing, and it was wrenched off in front of him, everybody got vague, and said, Well, now! How about a dough-nut! Or some coleslaw?

Tuck was trying not to think about Daniel. Of course, he'd been trying not to think about Daniel most of his life, that was the kind of brothers they were, but this was different.

He was going to be very mad at himself if the only kind of brother he would ever have been was a rotten one.

He touched the embroidered jacket the bus driver wore. "You have the same initials as me. T.M.," he said.

"Yeah? You better drive good, then."

"You really gonna let me?"

"Said I would, didn't I?"

"You can't believe everything people tell you," Tuck told him.

"What am I—your parent? Believe me."

Tuck believed him. He kept his eyes fastened on the road, waiting for the straightaway. But there was something wrong here. None of the roads were straight. These roads were Figure Eights. "Who designed these roads?" said Tuck, frowning. Was this America? People drove on these windy little lanes? What were they, insane?

"Heidi, dear," said Mrs. Camp, "take this tray of hot food and drinks into the barn for the workers there."

She nodded and set off before she remembered why there were workers in the barn.

The barn was the morgue.

Body bags really were just bags. No matter who you were, no matter what condition your body was in, you were just zippered in, like a parcel. You were no Christmas present, shinny and beribboned; you were brown paper. Ready to be shipped.

She found she could turn her mind off, as if she had electrical connections from which she could take the fuse.

She was okay with the bodies as long as she did not look at the faces or hands. The legs were legs. The shirts were shirts. The backs were backs.

But the hands: they had gender. Bitten nails. Rings. Age spots. Some were small and childlike, hands that had not yet learned how to steer a crayon. The hands were a person, somebody for whom family waited at an airport, never to hold again.

And the faces: impossible: she could not look at the faces. She blurred them like true crime television programs where the criminal's features turn watery to prevent identification.

She looked at the bags, not the people going into them. The bags were huge. They could have stuck giraffes in those bags. "Why so large?" she whispered.

"Sometimes," said the attendant, "you don't get the victim in until after rigor mortis, and the arms or the trunk can be twisted out and rigid, and you have to have—"

"Don't tell me any more," said Heidi. The body bag was plastic, with the longest zipper in the world. Somewhere out there is a factory, she thought, that makes body-bag zippers. Can you imagine doing that for a living? Inserting . . .

The girl they were zipping into the body bag was bloody from the chest down. She wore a lovely forest green sweater with large gleaming silver buttons on which little raised hearts held hands. A silver chain fell lopsidedly around her neck, and there was something on the chain—a charm, or a heart, or a crystal, but Heidi could not see it. In her arms was cradled, like a baby, another sweater.

Carly! thought Heidi. Carly, Carly, Carly!

She tried to keep herself from looking at Carly's face, but that was too cowardly. Carly deserved more. Heidi had to do her the honor of looking.

She looked.

Carly's face was undamaged. Her hair was wet. The wet hair looked alive. The face did not. "Don't zip it," said Heidi. She felt frantic, horribly energized, as if her body had captured Carly's lost strength.

The attendants looked at her in surprise. "She's gone," said one gently. "Been gone for a while."

Been gone for a while, thought Heidi. Sounds like a mountain lovers' lament; *she's been gone for a while; she'll be back 'fore long.*

"We lost quite of few of 'em," said the attendant. "If the site had been better . . . " he said, slowly, wishfully. "No woods, no hill, no ice." He shrugged. He said to Heidi, "You okay?" Then he began to zip the bag, closing in the pretty sweater, the silver chain.

Carly was dead.

Heidi was afraid she would weep, or throw up, or run through the woods and over the hills and out of town, anything to get away from this horror. Not Carly, who was going home!

Lost. We lost her. Oh, Carly, where are you now? Are you lost? Carly, Carly, come back, don't zip it, don't zip it.

But he zipped it, and Carly was gone.


*Saturday: 8:59 P.M.*


Patrick saw her standing between the barn and the triage area. She looked so utterly defeated.

But we're winning, thought Patrick. We're getting everybody out, in spite of the chaos; we've gotten organized, we've beaten the fire, Life Star is making its fourth run.

He came up behind her. He did not know why she would be in school with him this year. Super-rich kids occasionally popped up, usually because they were thrown out of private school for drugs or shoplifting, although drugs were so common now, even the best schools usually pretended not to see. They'd have no student body if they really focused on drug use.

Her face was a study in misery.

Patrick put his arms around her. "Hey," he said, not gently or softly because there was so much racket going on he had to shout; chainsaw, engines, helicopters, sirens of departing ambulances, walkie-talkies, portable phones, radios. "Hey, what's wrong?" he shouted.

She shrugged.

"Who died?" he said, pointing with his mud-stained toe toward the body bags. You're sick, Patrick, he thought, those're people in there, people you're pointing to with your sneaker.

"A girl our age. Carly. Somebody gave her a charm for her silver necklace. Her boyfriend, do you think? Or her parents? She was going home, Patrick."

He realized that she was sobbing.

"Going home," she said again. "She told me. She wanted to get there."

His arms tightened around her and he rocked her slightly, feeling like a physician with his patient, or a lover with his former love. He knew she would never really take the EMT training course. Fire and Ambulance volunteers were always working-type people, not rich-type people. And even if she wanted to, her parents would never let her. They'd let her play polo or tennis or whatever it was rich kids did this year, but they'd never let her hang out at an ambulance barn.

"The man over there," said Heidi, gulping, "told me if this was a better place, without a fountain wrecking up the courtyard, and no trees, no hills, no ice . . ."

Patrick said, "You're responsible for the site the plane crashed into? Get real, Heidi. Look at it this way. What if you lived in a shack? You're keeping a couple hundred people warm and fed. You're providing electricity and phones and water. You called in the alarm. What if it happened without you? What if nobody saw it come down? What if these rescue personnel were still looking just to find the plane? What if they had to bulldoze a whole damn *road* in to reach the plane, never mind taking away a few holly bushes?"

"She died, though," said Heidi.

He said, "You're fantastic, Heidi. You've done a million things to help save people tonight."

How callous I am, he thought. I don't know yet that this is real; I'm still an excited kid in the midst of the action. I'm wired. I'm the one who's flying here.

I'm having fun.

He tried to be horrified by his feelings but it didn't happen. He went on being incredibly glad that he had been first on the scene, that he had come through, that he got to be one of the helpers.

She said, "There's a little boy in one of those bags."

He did not know what to say to her. He struggled to think of something comforting, like—you were brilliant, thinking up the horse-stall door for our bridge—but she didn't care about bridges right now.

Patrick's father yelled, "Hey! You two necking over there? Save it!"

Heidi and Patrick looked at each other.

Patrick's father yelled. "Get your—uhhh—get up here! I got work for you two."

"He was about to tell me what part of my body I should get in gear," said Patrick, grinning. "Then he decided not to."

"Both of us need to get in gear," said Heidi. "I don't know what I'm doing in Neutral when I have to stay in High."

A spotlight caught her; the sopping hair gleamed, the cold ice-reddened cheeks tilted toward him; a smile of mischief teased him.

For an entire five or six seconds, he thought about sex instead of rescue.

# Twelve

Mr. MacArthur participated regularly in road races; every morning before breakfast he ran eight miles. He was proud of his physique.

But when the airline personnel had led them to the hotel, he had hardly been able to manage the walk. There had been an upward slope to the corridor. It seemed to him that wheelchairs were going to be necessary if he were to negotiate this hill. How could they build a public-access building with hills?

He thought, *Daniel.*

He thought, *Tuck.*

They're going to tell us the plane crashed, he thought. They want us safely away from the thousands of other passengers and the people picking them up. When we start screaming and sobbing and saying NO NO NO NO! they want us behind thick walls and closed doors. They want us together, to make it easier for them.

*Daniel.*

*Tuck.*

Were they scared? Did they know what was happening? Did it hurt? Did they feel themselves fall? How many minutes or seconds did they have, feeling it, knowing it, being terrified?

He thought of falling. Falling thousands and thousands of feet. What if you did not lose consciousness? What if you were alive to see the earth rushing toward you? What if you had time to know what was happening?

My baby boys, he thought, seeing them blindly, seeing them at all their ages at the same time: from birth to death; from sleeping to baseball pitching.

Not my sons, he thought. Not Tuck. Not Daniel.

*Saturday:* 9:01 P.M.

The plane, Teddie's mother told herself, had to land in some other city. Developed engine trouble. They've landed safely hundreds of miles from here and alternative arrangements are being made. Teddie is sitting right now in some stewardess's lap, having ice cream, being silly, having fun, being spoiled.

The plane is fine.

It has to be fine.

Teddie is on it.

So it's fine.

I won't listen to what that woman is saying. She's wrong. They're all wrong. They're making it up. My daughter is fine.

Something dripped onto her chest.

She looked down, surprised to be wet. They weren't outdoors. Was something leaking? Was—

She was crying, silently, effortlessly; her face was wet, her own tears were coming like rain, multiplying, like terror.


*Saturday:* 9:02 P.M.

In the hotel ballroom, folding chairs had been brought out. The chairs had metal frames and indigo blue backs and seats. Nobody had been willing to sit. Sitting was casual. They could not sit for this news.

"We have," said the neutrally voiced woman, "a partial list of survivors."

Several hundred people in the ballroom froze, or shuddered, or trembled. They did not speak or moan.

They leaned toward her, willing their sons or daughters, their mothers or fathers, their wives or husbands, their lovers or room-mates, to be on the survivor list.

"If you do not hear the name you are waiting for," said the woman, "it does not necessarily mean anything."

It means everything, thought Mr. MacArthur. It means death. That's what you are when you're not a survivor. You're dead.

He could not believe this.

Daniel. Tuck.

No.

Their names would be spoken right away, he'd phone them, he'd drive anywhere on earth to get them, they were fine. Probably hungry.

"Harrison, Tanya. Wysocki, Brad. Rochette, Valerie."

They'd get a pizza together. He and Daniel and Tuck. That's what they would do. He and his sons.

"DiNolica, Karen. Fitch, George. Serra, Richard. Gutierrez, Janet."

Little moans spurted out around him like blood from wounds. People began crying out. "Where are they? Where do we go? Are they in hospitals? Are they hurt at all? How do we—"

Stop talking! his heart screamed. I can't hear the list! Don't you understand, my sons' names are coming up! Stop talking!

But the talking had begun, and now everybody was talking, calling out the name they cared about: names, names, names, being shouted.

Because that's all that's left, he thought.

Names.

The voice was endless.

He prayed it would really be endless.

That the list of survivors would be the entire list of passengers.

The plane had not really crashed, just came down in the wrong place.

Everybody had walked away.

"Belter, Shannon. Fazzolo, Maria. MacArthur, Tucker."

"Tuck," he said out loud.

"Tuck!" he said again.

He grabbed the arm of the person near him. It was an airline person; he recognized that uniform. "Tuck," shouted Mr. MacArthur. He shook the airline man's arm vigorously. "Tuck survived!" he yelled. He could not understand why the entire room was not celebrating. Why were they telling him to be quiet? Didn't they understand? *Tuck had survived.*

The person walked Mr. MacArthur to the edge of the room. "Sir, could you tell me your relationship to Tucker MacArthur?" He had steered Mr. MacArthur so that they were facing the wall. There was flocked wallpaper on the wall: a sort of seasick blue, with icy velvetine flowers.

"I'm his father," he whispered. He had lost his voice. He cleared his throat several times, but his voice did not come back. The boys had been sitting together. And if you were not on the survivor list . . . Daniel was not on the survivor list . . . then . . . you were . . .

"Yes, sir." The man wrote on a legal pad.

"I have another son."

"Sir?"

"On the flight."

"Sir?"

"Daniel. Daniel MacArthur. They were sitting next to each other."

The man said. "We'll have to wait on that, sir. We have no information on that yet, sir."

He had not been called sir this many times in his life.

He studied the pattern of the seasick-blue wallpaper.

That's what they do when your kid dies, he thought. They call you sir.

*Saturday: 9:20 P.M.*

"That is the incomplete," said the neutral woman, "let me stress . . . *incomplete* . . . list of survivors. Remember . . . that rescue . . . is on-going," said the neutral woman. She paused even longer. She turned a little to the left and then a little to the right, taking them all into her gaze. Then she returned to her clipboard. She said, "Now I am going to ask the family of Bart Chase . . . if they will join this officer." She pointed to another neutral man, holding the same clipboard, the same list.

The family of Bart Chase did not appear. Nobody had been waiting for Bart Chase.

*Saturday: 9:21 P.M.*

Shirl thought, Bart Chase was probably going on a business trip. Bart Chase probably has a Monday morning appointment and won't be missed until then. Bart Chase probably has a wife and kids back home, but they rented a video, and they just finished popping popcorn, and they don't know.

O Family of Bart Chase, Shirl thought, tears stabbing her eyes, you'll know in the morning, they'll tell you in the morning.

She said to herself, It was an incomplete list of survivors.

Very incomplete.

Because my sister . . .

"Family of Carly Foyle," said the woman.

Shirley could feel her own hair. It was so odd, the way she could feel her hair: the extra hairspray, the heavy curls, the different part, so that she would look just right to see Carly.

It seemed pointless to walk through the crowd, greet the neutral woman, hear the neutral announcement.

There would be no reunion.

No forgiveness.

No more fights.

No more anything.

Because there was no more Carly.

And yet Shirl was moving. She stepped forward. She made progress. Around her, people moved out of her way. People stepped back for her as if she were a celebrity.

Nobody in the entire room seemed to be talking.

Shirl meant to say, "You made a mistake. You have Carly Foyle on the wrong list." But she said, "Did it hurt? Was she scared? What happened?" Shirl's voice crept up and up and up. "What happened? Was my sister scared?" screamed Shirl. "Where is she?"

She heard herself screaming, she knew she was hysterical, she knew this was not polite. She should not subject people to this.

She thought, Carly would behave better.

She thought, Carly is dead.

"Carly is dead?" she whispered to the neutral man.

He said, "I'm so sorry, miss."

# Thirteen

*Saturday: 10:48* P.M.

In the courtyard, a fight was going on.

The fire chief from Nearing River, who had taken charge from Patrick's father, was outraged because the FAA had arrived, and the inspectors were trying to take control of the scene away from him. The men were actually duking it out, sparring as if the pretty court-yard were a stone boxing ring. Patrick stared at them. Had he really wanted to do exactly the same thing himself only a few hours ago?

He did not want to act like that—the moron wasting time fighting somebody on his own team, especially when there was still work to be done.

Patrick walked away.

The place was ablaze with lights: lights that flashed in rows, spun in circles, whipped in blinding patterns: blue for firemen, yellow for tow trucks, green for ambulance responders, white strobes for the fire chief, red pulses for the police. His vision throbbed. Everywhere he turned were screaming sirens and leaping lights. It was hard to think or hear or see.

His scanner talked continually, but he could not both decipher the static-y messages and think, so he ignored the scanner and struggled on his own.

The biggest problem now was sightseers.

People had come from miles around, parking all along the narrow, inaccessible roads, hiking through the woods, poking over the scene, as if they wanted souvenirs, memories, participation.

The police had a man at each door to Dove House to keep the people inside safe from intrusion and to prevent the souvenir takers from starting on Heidi's family possessions.

The food in Dove House was long ago consumed. Eventually even the coleslaw found takers. When the Red Cross arrived with a truck of sandwiches, coffee, and orange juice, they were stormed. There was nothing like a rescue to make you hungry.

Patrick was tired.

So tired. He liked to work out; a couple of hours of weights, treadmill, and rowing machine was nothing.

But he had never ever been this tired. Tired like old people, thought Patrick. This must be what it's like to be Granddad. He can hardly get his foot high enough for a stair tread. That's how I feel.

Heidi was coming up the hill. It must be her thousandth trip. She looked as if she needed a tow rope this time. She was carrying her own blankets back from the helicopter, having traded them for the blankets on board. She had obviously fallen in the mud. Both she and her blankets looked as if they had been mining for coal.

Patrick found himself grinning. Possessively, as if Heidi were part of him, and he of her.

Patrick's father said to him, "You could do worse."

"Huh?"

"The girl. She's a cutie."

"You just think that because she doesn't fall apart in a crisis."

"I like that in a person," said his father. Slowly he took off his gear, stretched, let out a huge puff of exhaustion, and ate another doughnut. "I'm proud of you, son," said Patrick's father.

They looked at each other. Patrick felt sober and awed.

Then he laughed. "I loved it, Dad."

His father nodded. "We all do. There's an excitement to rescue that nothing else has. You don't want an accident, but if there is one, you sure want to be in on it."

They both headed for Heidi, but they weren't first in line. An FAA official stopped her. Sternly, as if he were her truant officer. "It is my understanding that you both heard and saw the plane crash, Miss Landseth," said the official. "Tell me about it. What exactly happened? Precisely." He had a large clipboard and was poised to take down everything useful that she said.

Heidi shrugged with both her hands and her shoulders, apologizing with her posture. "I don't know."

Patrick hated how she apologized for herself. It was a habit he definitely wanted her to quit.

"What time was it?" said the FAA official. "Exactly? Do you know?"

We weren't in that time zone, thought Patrick, we weren't in a place where time is exact. Some of it raced past, time in which people were dying. But the very same time gathered slowly, when our hands struggled, our feet slipped, and no progress was made.

What progress had they made?

How many people had they saved and how many had they lost?

How many had died on impact? How many were doing well at hospitals across the state? Would he ever know what had happened to them? Or would his part in this operation be yet a third sort of time? A stranded, unattached time, with no past and no future: just a motion, setting people on stretchers and watching them leave.


*Saturday: 10:49* P.M.

They loaded Daniel into the helicopter.

"You're last, kid," said the attendant, grinning, putting a blood-pressure cuff around his arm.

"That was pretty lousy of you," said Daniel. "I wanted to go first."

"You should have," said the doctor, or the paramedic, or whoever he was. Probably just a passerby, thought Daniel. Probably they used up all the real ones with the first trips. This guy just picked up a white coat and climbed in.

"They had to cut you out, huh?" said the attendant.

Daniel meant to say yes, but he was getting woozy again, he'd been woozy all through the cutting out, although Mrs. Jemmison said he was doing fine, everything was fine, the whole thing was coming along just fine; he'd wanted to say, Mrs. Jemmison, are you on drugs? This is not fine.

Daniel felt the helicopter lift, felt himself lifting at a different pace, his soul and his inner organs shifting position, as if trying to decide whether to stick together. Or maybe it was the helicopter shifting. It would really be the pits if the helicopter crashed.

He thought, I'll make a joke; tell these guys we all need a laugh about now.

But his lips didn't go along with it. They didn't say anything.

The colors of his enclosed world flashed for a moment like sunlight on the beach and then faded.

Heidi looked down at her watch. I used to know what time it happened, she thought. I was clocking those first few minutes. But I don't know anymore. It was a hundred years ago.

The weird thing was, it had not crossed her mind to wonder what had caused the crash.

The inspector seemed not to believe this. "You've been working here for hours," he said, "you must have thought back on what you first heard and saw."

But she had not thought back at all. She had only thought ahead, trying to guess the right thing to do next. "Doesn't the radar tell you that?" she said. "Don't you find a little black box somewhere that records what happened?"

"I'm asking for your description," he said.

She had no description. "Whatever went wrong, though," said Heidi, "had to have gone wrong before they were in my backyard. We don't normally have planes circle above us here."

She saw somebody carrying bodies as if they were baggage, by the handles, and at first she was shocked and angry, until she realized it really was baggage, and incredibly enough they were rescuing that, too. "Are all the people out of the plane now?" she said to him.

He seemed uncomfortable with the question.

Somebody else said, "We didn't get anybody in the cockpit. Maybe in the morning. And beyond the ravine, there are maybe thirty or forty bodies we haven't retrieved."

"And who knows how many in the burned wing section," added another man.

"We're done with Life Star, though. Nobody left alive to tow off."

"God, that was a bad site, where we had to load the helicopter. Barbed wire around the whole damn field."

"It was a pasture," said Heidi faintly. There had to be a fence around a pasture.

"Yeah, well, somebody might have mentioned the barbed wire. You can't see it in the dark. We ran into it. But somebody had his toolbox in his truck, wire clippers, we got it down, rolled up, but not without a bunch of people getting scraped up something fierce."

Heidi found herself crying and then found Patrick's arm around her, for what—the third time that night? "She's gonna be okay, I think," said Patrick. "By now she's gotta be at a hospital already."

"Huh?" said Heidi.

"Teddie." He was smiling at her, concerned, but now she really could not stop crying because now she was even worse; she had forgotten about Teddie again. Patrick's huge, dirty fingers smoothed her tears away, matching gestures for each cheek. He kissed her forehead. "Let's get some coffee," he said. "You need to warm up."

"Actually I hate coffee," she said.

"Me, too. But I keep thinking one of these days I'm going to see why other people like it. Let's give it a try."

"We can't stop working," she said fearfully.

"Yeah, we can, actually," he said. "There are hundreds of people here now, Heidi. Some of them haven't contributed anything at all yet. Give them a turn."

"First I want to look again for Tally-Ho, our fourth dog," said Heidi.

Patrick was pretty sure he had seen the dog. He almost told her what had happened to Tally and decided not to. It could, like a lot of other things, wait until morning. Shrapnel from a splitting plane did ugly things.

"Later," he said to her, trying to make his voice expansive and comfortable, like his father's.


*Saturday: 10:58 p.m.*

Mr. Farquhar yawned hugely, several times. "Let's watch the eleven o'clock news, kids. We'll be on it. Might as well see what the media got wrong."

"What can you get wrong about a plane crash?" said Patrick. Sometimes his father really irritated him. Patrick loved television, and his father was cynical about it. "Come on, Heid," he said, taking her hand.

A nickname. Nicknames meant affection. They were friends. Whatever else had happened on this terrible night, Heidi had made friends. She didn't want to give him a nickname, though. Patrick was such a nice name. She didn't want to say Pat.

"Let's go watch ourselves," said Patrick.

Heidi was doubtful about television, though. The crash was pretty clear in her mind. She didn't need to see a film of it.

But Patrick kept her hand and led the way. The warmth of Dove House enveloped them, and the very different, incredibly comforting warmth of his hand was something she never wanted to surrender. I should have held Carly's hand longer, thought Heidi. Hand holding is everything.

She and Patrick and Mr. Farquhar and Robyn and Gorp went into the little room off the kitchen, where a small TV sat cozily on a shelf. Mrs. Camp usually sat there to crochet one of her hideous blankets. In fact, Mrs. Camp was there right now, sound asleep, wrapped in coats, as all the blankets had been used. Heidi loved her, thinking, What a great family I have. Thinking, I'm the one who has to talk to Carly's sister. Tell her Carly was coming home. At least she was aimed right, even if she didn't make it.

Heidi wept.

The eleven o'clock news began.

They listened to the voice of the reporter as the camera flicked over crash and plane, woods and house. The filming gave little idea of the hugeness of the crashed plane. It was just a big white thing in the dark. Not the horrifying two story-high nightmare she had been passing all night.

If anything, the cameraman had been more taken by Dove House than by the 747; he managed to have it in most of his shots.

The camera panned down the length of the Gallery, catching the fine marble, now patchy with bloodstains. The camera contrasted the beautiful paintings on the wall to the horror of two body bags awaiting removal to the barn. It focused on a discarded bandage wrapper and slid into the Hall, filled, when they were filming, with the last of the hurt passengers and exhausted but still wired rescuers. In the corner, Heidi was shocked to see the afghan twitching. Teddie had been there even then, unnoticed by anybody, rescuer or cameraman.

The anchorwoman, amoral in her flawless beauty, held a microphone, like a lover, to her lips. Facing the camera with a sober, serious expression, she said, "Darienne, how does it feel to be one of the survivors of this terrible tragedy?"

I let her do this, thought Heidi. I should have rammed the dogs down her throat and been done with all of them.

Darienne, too, faced the camera, her lovely face as impeccable as the anchorwoman's, her hair as unruffled, her eyes as beautifully made up. She said gravely, "This has been a desperate hour for me. In helping the wounded, in bringing food and water to the sick, in holding the hands of the dying, I have become a better person."

"Why, that scum bucket," said Patrick. He almost had a heart attack from pure rage. "Dad, she's the one who wouldn't so much as pour coffee. She was up there in Heidi's own bathroom using Heidi's blowdryer to fix her hair when people were down here dying. Dad, get a kitchen knife. We've got to find her. Stab that girl."

His father laughed. "Now, Patrick. We can't be both life-savers and life-takers."

"I don't know why not. Does she deserve to breathe? Look at her, getting fame and air time when all around her, people are dead and dying!"

On the news, Darienne lifted her chin bravely. A single tear crept down her pale cheek. She whispered. "I am privileged to be here among these selfless and giving people."

"I bet she's a thief, too," said Patrick. "Make a cop search her. I bet she lifted jewelry."

His father took Patrick's upper arm firmly. "She doesn't matter. Anyway, what have I told you about television news? It's never right."

"Dad! She does matter! She's the one who's on TV!" Patrick resisted his father, and for a minute they were two large, muscled men going in opposite directions.

But he was still seventeen, and he was still used to obeying, and his resistance faded. "Okay, okay, I won't kill her."

"Anyway she's not here anymore," said Robyn. "She paid somebody to give her a ride to wherever she's going."

"Probably your money, Heidi," said Patrick darkly. "She probably fished around under your mattress and that's what's paying for her ride. The scum."

Heidi giggled. "I don't keep money under my mattress, and if I did, Patrick, I can't think of a better use for it than getting Darienne off my estate." Her laugh was sweet and silvery.

Patrick said, "They should have filmed you, Heidi."

# Fourteen

"This is my second quarter, actually," said Teddie. "I lost my real one when the plane crashed."

The nurse nodded. "Well, we've made the phone call for you, sweetheart, so you can hang onto your second quarter. Here's Mommy. She's pretty nervous, so you make her feel better, you hear me? And then it's straight back to bed."

Teddie smiled and took the phone. "Hi, Mommy. I've been trying to call you."

Her mother said Teddie's name about twenty times.

Teddie said, "Mommy, I'm fine. I did good. Everybody told me so. You don't have to worry. It's just a little old break in my leg. And I have a great big cast. And I'm staying overnight here. I have my own room and everything. 'Course I'm not in my room now, because I'm sitting on the nurses' station. They call it a station, but it's really a shelf, like a big kitchen, with telephones. I didn't need my quarter. They made the phone call for me."

Her mother said her name another twenty times.

Teddie said, "*And* I flew in a helicopter. And *it* didn't crash."

Now her father was saying her name over and over.

Teddie said, "*And* I have a bracelet with my name on it. *Plus*, they blew up a nurses glove like a balloon and drew smily faces on each of the fingers."

"So you're okay," said her father.

"No. I'm terribly badly, very badly, horribly badly, hurt."

The nurse said, "Let me talk now, Teddie."

*Sunday:* 12:20 A.M.

"You know how we left the site, Dad?" said Tuck. "On a school bus. This kid that was driving it? You know what? He let me drive for a few minutes."

His father could hardly hold the phone. Shudders of relief extended to the tips of his fingers. But parental scolding triumphed. "Tuck! You're thirteen years old!"

"I know," said Tuck reverently. "It was on a straightaway, though, Dad," he assured his father.

His father moaned. "That's like turning the plane over to the janitor."

"It is not! I steered fine. And nobody on the school bus complained. They all clapped."

"That's probably because they're happy about the amount of money they're going to sue me for," said his father, thinking of ice and darkness and people who had just escaped a plane crash now being in a bus crash.

"Dad," said Tuck. "You have an attitude problem these days, you know. Well, listen, I have to hang up and call Mom. Say hi to Linda. Tell her we're sorry we'll miss the wedding."

"Yeah, I bet. You two probably staged the whole plane crash."

Tuck tried to laugh.

Only somebody who had never seen a plane crash could say that. Somebody who had not slipped and slid across an icy field while his fellow passengers burned to death.

Tuck said, "I love you, Dad."

It wasn't a sentence he had expected to use again in this lifetime. But he was among the one third of the four hundred passengers to survive—a high number, people said, for a plane crash. And Tuck felt he had been given a second lifetime.

Daniel was in surgery.

So they said.

Tuck hadn't seen him yet. But the doctor did not seem like the fibbing type, although you never knew with adults. The doctor had said he thought Daniel would make it, and Tuck had said suspiciously, "Make it how? Crippled?" and the doctor said, "No, I think he'll play ball again. Eventually." And smiled and went into surgery.

So Tuck was banking on that. That Daniel would get another lifetime, too.

"Nothing to worry about, Dad," said Tuck. "We're survivors, Daniel and me." He wondered what Daniel would say if he were on the phone with Dad, and immediately he knew exactly what Daniel would say, and so he said it. "After all, Dad, we've been through a divorce. What's a plane crash compared to that?"

*Sunday: 12:25 A.M.—*
*Nearing River, Connecticut*
*6:25 A.M.—Geneva, Switzerland*

"My daughter?" repeated Alex Landseth.

Mr. Farquhar was irritated with the man. "Yes, your daughter," he said impatiently. "Heidi. Splendid girl. Cool in a crisis. Tremendous help. You don't have a thing to worry about with this kid."

There was a moment of silence, as if Landseth was thinking of some other Heidi. Then he said, "Thank you."

Patrick's father shook his head. So many parents seemed not to have pride in their own kids. He couldn't imagine it. Especially not with this little girl. What a head she had on her shoulders! He changed the subject. "The chaos at your house is pretty unbelievable, Mr. Landseth. The plane ripped out wood, fences, landscaping, and the rescue vehicles ripped out a lot more. Heidi gave us permission to use the house as center of operations and medical treatment center. Now the thing is, your place is crawling with airline personnel, safety personnel, fire personnel. But no wounded are left, and there's no worry about fire now. I'm taking Heidi on home with me to spend the night because she can't sleep here. Mrs. Camp's daughter came for her, and she's spending the night in New Canaan. The police will have people here, so don't worry about the safety of the house." He gave the man his home number. He added, "Heidi's a doll. I'm really looking forward to meeting her parents." He wasn't, particularly, but that was the kind of thing you said to let people know you liked their kid.

Mr. Landseth said, "Is Heidi there? May I speak to her?"

"Heidi!" bellowed Patrick's father. "Talk to your father."

Heidi took the phone. She was glowing. "Daddy!" she said bursting. "I have so many things to tell you. It's been the most incredible night. Daddy, I was really useful."

Alex Landseth sat in Switzerland.

*Useful.*

As if that were the most wonderful thing on earth: to be useful.

Perfect hair, slim ankles, smooth complexion, high grades, captain of this, honors in that—nice enough in their way.

But to be *useful*.

From her tone of voice, *useful* was better than anything.

"I'm so proud of you," said her father huskily.

His daughter's silvery laugh, so rare because her parents had not often been proud, trembled across the Atlantic Ocean.


*Sunday: 12:40* A.M.—
*Nearing River, Connecticut*
*Saturday: 9:40* P.M.—*San Diego, California*

"But you're all right," said her mother again.

"I told you, Mom. I'm fine."

"You didn't get hit or burned or anything."

"No, Mom, I'm fine."

"We have been trying for *hours* to get through to you."

"I know, Mom. But I was too busy to talk anyway."

"I wouldn't have wanted you to see any of that," said her mother.

"You couldn't have stopped it," said Heidi. "This is where the plane came down."

"You'll have nightmares," said her mother. "Are you sure you're all right, Heidi-eidi-O?"

"I'm sure I'm all right." She rolled her eyes at Patrick, who rolled his back. Parents.

"I'm flying to Connecticut in the morning," said her mother.

"Mom. Take a bus."

"*A bus?*" said Rebecca Landseth, truly horrified.

"Mom, I love you, okay? I don't want you to crash."

"I would rather take my statistical chances," said Rebecca Landseth, "than ever set foot on a bus. Now, who are these people you said you're spending the night with? I mean, can you trust them?"


*Sunday: 12:48* A.M.

The FAA was putting up yellow plastic ribbons, cordoning off each section, keeping people out. You could still see some of the victims, waiting, but they were not waiting to be resuscitated. They were waiting to be buried. Video cameras rolled, and regular cameras flashed. They were immortalizing the crash, getting it on tape, to be analyzed, like ash and bone. To find out what went wrong.

She did not need a tape. She had it in her brain. I will play this in my head for the rest of my life. If I live to be ninety or if I die like Carly—so young—this will be mine, this will be me, this will never let go.

Heidi said to the inspector, "Do you know yet what caused the crash?"

He looked at her with pity for her stupidity and ignorance. In the wisdom Heidi had gathered from this terrible night, she realized this was the only expression his face had. It was probably why he held the job—so he could look superior. Poor thing, she thought. He's just an ankle biter like Winnie and Clemmie.

"The Dove House crash is very interesting," said the FAA inspector.

Interesting? thought Heidi. That's the best word he could come up with?

"A plane crash is not usually a mass casualty incident," added the inspector.

"Incident?" repeated Heidi. As if it were the same as doing wheelies on the school lawn. "What do you mean?"

The inspector was the kind of person who loved to put things in simple terms, to show how simpleminded you were not to have understood in the first place. "Mass casualty," he said condescendingly, "is injuries. A lot of hurt people. You don't usually have that with a plane crash."

Heidi could not grasp what he was saying. How could you not have a lot of hurt people? Of course they'd be hurt.

"They're usually all dead," said the inspector.

What if they had all died?

Could she spend another night here if her barn had been nothing but body bags? Could she call the Dove House—doves, the symbol of peace—if four hundred people had died in its shadow? Could anybody ride a pony, pick a yellow rose, or walk along the reflecting pool if what was reflected was the end of four hundred innocent lives?

She thought of the little girl: Teddie: Teddie's quarter.

She thought, Somewhere in my grass is Teddie's quarter, like a tiny, round gravestone.

She prayed that Teddie was all right. She thought of Carly and wondered if death was all right: if Carly was safe. She reached out blindly for a hand to hold again and ended up with Patrick's father's.

He grinned at her and transferred her to Patrick. Heidi blushed. "You've done this a lot, haven't you, Mr. Farquhar?" she said, trying to rescue herself.

"No, thank God," he said. "I've never done this before. Nobody here has ever done this before."

"But you knew what you were doing."

"Not really. We were doing exactly what you did, Heidi. Lurching forward. Hoping to be right. We get mass casualty training, of course. In case the nuclear plant goes. In case there's a chemical fire at the factory. In case the school bus crashes." He sighed. "But I didn't feel very trained, for sure."

They stood in the courtyard, in the astonishing amount of debris that had accumulated from the rescue efforts. Heidi thought momentarily of what it was going to take to clean up, to dismantle and get rid of the 747 body, and dismissed the problem. Much too much to think of now.

"Let's go home, kids," said Mr. Farquhar.

Heidi thought of Carly again. Of going home. She circled Patrick's chest with her arms and wept there, as if he were not a person, but a wailing wall, like the one in Jerusalem. After a long time she heard his heart, thudding regularly. A living heart. She listened to it, and then to her own heart keeping time with his. They were both alive. They had both done the best they could.

Patrick said, "My mom fixed the guest room for you at our house." He said, "Get a change of clothes and we're heading home."

"I could never sleep," said Heidi, but she knew that she would; that her terrific overdosing energy had sapped her like chemotherapy, that she would sleep for hours, in any bed.

They walked slowly toward Patrick's truck. They did not look back. And strangely, they did not have to hold each other up. They were, in some terrible unfair way, stronger than they had been eight hours ago.

Built by death and suffering, thought Heidi. She said to him, "We're alive."

He nodded, tightening his grip on her hand. What a great thing a hand was. He thought, I'm starving. I hope Mom has something to eat.

His mother always had something to eat. They were an eating family. There was nothing like food. He said. "You like spaghetti? Steak? Hamburgers? Or are you in a pancake mood? Sausage? Syrup?"

"I could eat all of that," said Heidi.

He was suddenly so tired he wondered if he was going to be able to drive home. His eyes drooped, his feet stumbled, his brain began to shut down.

He looked at Heidi. He thought, I'd rather be dead on the plane than ask a girl to drive me. A grin showed up on his face. A little energy returned.

"What's funny?" said Heidi, smiling, too, ready to share it.

He'd never share it.

He said, "Race you to the truck."

"What, are you insane? I couldn't race a falling leaf. I'll be lucky if I even reach the truck."

He thought mundanely that life went on. You could be at a plane crash and still fall in love. You could see death and mutilation and still want spaghetti. He patted his pocket, and his heart lurched. You could be a hero and still not be able to find your car keys.

There they were. Other pocket. If he had lost his car keys in this mess, years could go by before he located them again.

"Keys," he said to Heidi triumphantly.

"Home, driver," she said.

He thought, Heidi. It's a nice name.

He thought maybe he would boost her up when they got to the truck. He thought it would be nice if she stayed several days. He thought . . . *Dear God, I'm glad I'm alive.*

# Related Readings

*from*

# A Night to Remember

Walter Lord

## *You Go and I'll Stay a While*

*On April 14, 1912, the* Titanic, *a luxury ocean liner thought to be unsinkable, struck an iceberg and sank on her maiden voyage. More than 1,500 people lost their lives in what is one of the most famous disasters in modern history.*

SECOND CLASS PASSENGER Lawrence Beesley considered himself the rankest landlubber, but even he knew what rockets meant. The *Titanic* needed help—needed it so badly she was calling on any ship near enough to see.

The others on the Boat Deck understood too. There was no more joking or lingering. In fact, there was hardly time to say good-by.

"It's all right, little girl," called Dan Marvin to his new bride; "you go and I'll stay a while." He blew her a kiss as she entered the boat.

"I'll see you later," Adolf Dyker smiled as he helped Mrs. Dyker across the gunwale.

"Be brave; no matter what happens, be brave," Dr. W. T. Minahan told Mrs. Minahan as he stepped back with the other men.

Mr. Turrell Cavendish said nothing to Mrs. Cavendish. Just a kiss . . . a long look . . . another kiss . . . and he disappeared into the crowd.

Mark Fortune took his wife's valuables, as he and his son Charles saw off Mrs. Fortune and their three daughters. "I'll take care of them;

we're going in the next boat," he explained. "Charles, take care of Father," one of the girls called back to her brother.

"Walter, you must come with me," begged Mrs. Walter D. Douglas.

"No," Mr. Douglas replied, turning away, "I must be a gentleman."

"Try and get off with Major Butt and Mr. Moore," came a final bit of wifely advice; "They are big, strong fellows and will surely make it."

Some of the wives still refused to go. Mr. and Mrs. Edgar Meyer of New York felt so self-conscious arguing about it in public that they went down to their cabin. There, they decided to part on account of their baby.

Arthur Ryerson had to lay down the law to Mrs. Ryerson: "You must obey orders. When they say 'Women and children to the boats,' you *must* go when your turn comes. I'll stay here with Jack Thayer. We'll be all right."

Alexander T. Compton, Jr., was just as firm when his mother announced she would stay rather than leave him behind: "Don't be foolish, Mother. You and Sister go in the boat—I'll look out for myself."

Mr. and Mrs. Lucien Smith were having the same kind of argument. Seeing Captain Smith standing near with a megaphone, Mrs. Smith had an inspiration. She went up to him, explained she was all alone in the world, and asked if her husband could go along with her. The old Captain ignored her, lifted his megaphone and shouted, "Women and children first!"

At this point Mr. Smith broke in: "Never mind, Captain, about that; I'll see she gets in the boat." Turning to his wife, he spoke very slowly: " I never expected to ask you to obey, but this is one time you must. It is only a matter of form to have women and children first. The ship is thoroughly equipped and everyone on her will be saved."

Mrs. Smith asked him if he was being completely truthful. Mr. Smith gave a firm, decisive, "Yes." So they kissed good-by, and as the boat dropped to the sea, he called from the deck, "Keep your hands in your pockets; it is very cold weather."

Sometimes it took more than gentle deception. Mrs. Emil Taussig was clinging to her husband when No. 8 started down with her daughter. Mrs. Taussig turned and cried, "Ruth!" The brief distraction proved enough: two men tore her from Mr. Taussig and dropped her into the lowering boat.

A seaman yanked Mrs. Charlotte Collyer by the arm, another by her waist, and they dragged her from her husband Harvey. As she kicked to get free, she heard him call, "Go, Lottie! For God's sake, be brave and go! I'll get a seat in another boat!"

When Celiney Yasbeck saw she had to go alone, she began yelling and crying to rejoin Mr. Yasbeck, but the boat dropped to the sea while she tried in vain to get out.

No amount of persuasion or force could move Mrs. Hudson J. Allison of Montreal. A little apart from the rest, she huddled close to Mr. Allison, while their small daughter Lorraine tugged at her skirt.

Mrs. Isidor Straus also refused to go: "I've always stayed with my husband; so why should I leave him now?"

They had indeed come a long way together: the ashes of the Confederacy . . . the small china business in Philadelphia . . . building Macy's into a national institution . . . Congress . . . and now the happy twilight that crowned successful life—advisory boards, charities, hobbies, travel. This winter they had been to Cap Martin, and the *Titanic's* maiden voyage seemed a pleasant way to finish the trip.

Tonight the Strauses came on deck with the others, and at first Mrs. Straus seemed uncertain what to do. At one point she handed some small jewelry to her maid Ellen Bird, then took it back again. Later she crossed the Boat Deck and almost entered No. 8—then turned around and rejoined Mr. Straus. Now her mind was made up: "We have been living together for many years. Where you go, I go."

Archibald Gracie, Hugh Woolner, other friends tried in vain to make her go. Then Woolner turned to Mr. Straus: "I'm sure nobody would object to an old gentleman like you getting in . . . "

"I will not go before the other men," he said, and that was that. Then he and Mrs. Straus sat down together on a pair of deck chairs.

But most of the women entered the boats—wives escorted by their husbands, single ladies by the men who had volunteered to look out for them. This was the era when gentlemen formally offered their services to "unprotected ladies" at the start of an Atlantic voyage. Tonight the courtesy came in handy.

Mrs. William T. Graham, 19-year-old Margaret, and her governess Miss Shutes were helped into Boat 8 by Howard Case, London manager of Vacuum Oil, and young Washington Augustus Roebling, the steel heir who was striking out on his own as manager of the Mercer Automobile Works in Trenton, New Jersey. As No. 8 dropped to the sea, Mrs. Graham watched Case, leaning against the rail, light a cigarette and wave good-by.

Mrs. E. D. Appleton, Mr. R. C. Cornell, Mr. J. Murray Brown and Miss Edith Evans, returning from a family funeral in Britain, were under Colonel Gracie's wing, but somehow in the crowd he lost them, and it wasn't until much later that he found them again.

Perhaps the Colonel was distracted by his simultaneous efforts to look after Mrs. Churchill Candee, his table companion in the dining saloon. Mrs. Candee was returning from Paris to see her son, who had suffered the novelty of an airplane accident, and she must have been attractive indeed. Just about everybody wanted to protect her.

When Edward A. Kent, another table companion, found her after the crash, she gave him an ivory miniature of her mother for safe-keeping. Then Hugh Woolner and Bjornstrom Steffanson arrived and helped her into Boat 6. Woolner waved good-by, assuring her that they would help her on board again when the *Titanic* "steadied her-self." A little later Gracie and Clinch Smith dashed up, also in search of Mrs. Candee, but Woolner told them, perhaps a little smugly, that she had been cared for and was safely away.

It was just as well, for the slant in the deck was steeper, and even the carefree were growing uneasy. Some who left everything in their cabins now thought better of it and ventured below to get their valu-ables. They were in for unpleasant surprises. Celiney Yasbeck found her room was completely under water. Gus Cohen discovered the same thing. Victorine, the Ryersons' French maid, had an even more disturbing experience. She found her cabin still dry, but as she rum-maged about, she heard a key turn, suddenly realized the steward was locking the stateroom door to prevent looting. Her shriek was just in time to keep him from locking her in. Without stretching her luck any further, she dashed back on deck empty-handed.

Time was clearly running out. Thomas Andrews walked from boat to boat, urging the women to hurry: "Ladies, you *must* get in at once. There is not a moment to lose. You cannot pick and choose your boat. Don't hesitate. Get in, get in!"

Andrews had good reason to be exasperated. Women were never more unpredictable. One girl waiting to climb into No. 8 suddenly cried out. "I've forgotten Jack's photograph and must get it." Every-body protested, but she darted below. In a moment she reappeared with the picture and was rushed into the boat.

It was all so urgent—and yet so calm—that Second Officer Lightoller felt he was wasting time when Chief Officer Wilde asked him to help find the firearms. Quickly he led the Captain, Wilde, and First Officer Murdoch to the locker where they were kept. Wilde shoved one of the guns into Lightoller's hand, remarking, "You may need it." Lightoller stuck it in his pocket and hurried back to the boat.

One after another they now dropped rapidly into the sea: No. 6 at 12:55 . . . No. 3 at 1:00 . . . No. 8 at 1:10. Watching them go, First Class passenger William Carter advised Harry Widener to try for a boat. Widener shook his head: " I think I'll stick to the big ship, Billy, and take a chance."

Some of the crew weren't as optimistic. When Assistant Second Steward Wheat noticed Chief Steward Latimer wearing his lifebelt over his greatcoat, he urged the Chief to put it under the coat—this made swimming easier.

On the bridge, as Fourth Officer Boxhall and Quartermaster Rowe fired off more rockets, Boxhall still couldn't believe what was happening. "Captain," he asked, "is it *really* serious?"

"Mr. Andrews tells me," Smith answered quietly, "that he gives her from an hour to an hour and a half."

Lightoller had a more tangible yardstick—the steep, narrow emergency staircase that ran from the Boat Deck all the way down to E Deck. The water was slowly crawling up the stairs, and from time to time Lightoller walked over to the entrance and checked the number of steps it had climbed. He could see very easily, for the lights still gleamed under the pale green water.

His gauge showed time was flying. The pace grew faster—and sloppier. A pretty French girl stumbled and fell as she tried to climb into No. 9. An older woman in a black dress missed No. 10 entirely. She fell between the bow and the side of the ship. But as the crowd gasped, someone miraculously caught her ankle. Others hauled her into the Promenade Deck below, and she climbed back to the Boat Deck for another try. This time she made it.

Some of them lost their nerve. An old lady made a big fuss at No. 9, finally shook off everybody, and ran away from the boat altogether. A hysterical woman thrashed about helplessly, trying to climb into No. 11. Steward Witter stood on the rail to help her, but she lost her footing anyway, and they tumbled into the boat together. A large fat woman stood crying near No. 13: "Don't put me in the boat. I don't want to go into the boat! I have never been in an open boat in my life!"

Steward Ray brushed aside her protests—"You've got to go, and you may as well keep quiet."

A plan to fill some of the boats from the lower gangways went completely haywire. The doors that were to be used were never opened. The boats that were to stand by rowed off. The people who were to go were left stranded. When the Caldwells and several others went all the way down to a closed gangway on C Deck, somebody who didn't know about the plan locked the door behind them. Later some men on the deck above discovered the group and lowered a ladder for them to crawl back up.

A shortage of trained seamen made the confusion worse. Some of the best men had been used to man the early boats. Other old hands were off on special jobs—rounding up lanterns, opening the A Deck windows, helping fire the rockets. Six seamen were lost when they went down to open one of the lower gangways; they never came back . . . probably trapped far below. Now Lightoller was rationing the hands he had left—only two crewmen to a lifeboat.

No. 6 was halfway down when a woman called up to the Boat Deck, "We've only one seaman in the boat!"

"Any seamen there?" Lightoller asked the people on deck.

"If you like, I will go," called a voice from the crowd.

"Are you a seaman?"

"I am a yachtsman."

"If you're sailor enough to get out on that fall, you can go down." Major Arthur Godfrey Peuchen—vice-commodore of the Royal Canadian Yacht Club—swung himself out on the forward fall and slid down into the boat. He was the only male passenger Lightoller allowed in a boat that night.

Men had it luckier on the starboard side. Murdoch continued to allow them in if there was room. The French aviator Pierre Maréchal and sculptor Paul Chevré climbed into No. 7. A couple of Gimbels buyers reached No. 5. When the time came to lower No. 3, Henry Sleeper Harper not only joined his wife, but he brought along his Pekingese Sun Yat-sen and an Egyptian dragoman named Hamad Hassah, whom he had picked up in Cairo as a sort of joke.

On the same side, Dr. Washington Dodge was standing uncertainly in the shadow of No. 13, when Dining Room Steward Ray noticed him. Ray asked whether the doctor's wife and son were off, and Dodge said yes. Ray was relieved, because he took a personal interest in them. He had served the Dodges coming over on the *Olympic*. In fact, he had persuaded them to take the *Titanic* back. In a way, he was why the Dodges were on board . . . It was no time for philosophy—Ray called out, "You had better get in here," and he pushed the doctor into the boat.

The scene was almost punctilious at No. 1. Sir Cosmo Duff Gordon, his wife and her secretary Miss Francatelli—whom Lady Duff Gordon liked to call Miss Franks—asked Murdoch if they could enter.

"Oh certainly do; I'll be very pleased," Murdoch replied, according to Sir Cosmo. (On the other hand, Lookout George Symons, standing near, thought Murdoch merely said, "Yes, jump in.") Then two Americans, Abraham Solomon and C. E. H. Stengel, came up and were invited in too. Stengel had trouble climbing over the rail; finally got on top of it and rolled into the boat. Murdoch, an agile terrier of a man, laughed pleasantly, "That's the funniest thing I've seen tonight."

Nobody else seemed to be around—all the nearby boats were gone and the crowd had moved aft. When the five passengers were safely loaded, Murdoch added six stokers, put Lookout Symons in charge and told him, "Stand off from the ship's side and return when we call you." Then he waved to the men at the davits, and they lowered No. 1—capacity 40 persons—with exactly 12 people.

As the boat creaked down, Greaser Walter Hurst watched it from the forward well deck. He remembers observing somewhat caustically, "If they are sending the boats away, they might just as well put some people in them."

Down in Third Class there were those who didn't even have the opportunity to miss going in No. 1. A swarm of men and women milled around the foot of the main steerage staircase, all the way aft on E Deck. They had been there ever since the stewards got them up. At first there were just women and married couples; but then the men arrived from forward, pouring back along "Scotland Road" with their luggage. Now they were all jammed together—noisy and restless, looking more like inmates than passengers amid the low ceilings, the naked light bulbs, the scrubbed simplicity of the plain white walls.

Third Class Steward John Edward Hart struggled to get them into life jackets. He didn't have much luck—partly because he was also assuring them there was no danger, partly because many of them didn't understand English anyhow. Interpreter Muller did the best he could with the scores of Finns and Swedes, but it was slow going.

At 12:30 orders came down to send the women and children up to the Boat Deck. It was hopeless to expect them to find their way alone through the maze of passages normally sealed off from Third Class; so Hart decided to escort them up in little groups. This took time, too, but at last a convoy was organized and started off.

It was a long trip—up the broad stairs to the Third Class lounge on C Deck . . . across the open well deck . . . by the Second Class library and into First Class quarters. Then down the long corridor by the surgeon's office, the private saloon for the maids and valets of First Class passengers, finally up the grand stairway to the Boat Deck.

Hart led his group to Boat No. 8, but even then the job wasn't over. As fast as he got them in, they would jump out and go inside where it was warm.

It was after one o'clock when Hart got back to E Deck to organize another trip. It was no easier. Many women still refused to go. On the other hand, some of the men now insisted on going. But that was out of the question, according to the orders he had.

Finally he was off again on the same long trek. It was 1:20 by the time he reached the Boat Deck and led the group to No. 15. No time to go back for more. Murdoch ordered him into the boat and off he went with his second batch at about 1:30.

There was no hard-and-fast policy. One way or another, many of the steerage passengers avoided the *cul de sac* on E Deck and got topside. There they stood waiting, nobody to guide or help them. A few of the barriers that marked off their quarters were down. Those who came across these openings wandered into other parts of the ship. Some eventually found their way to the Boat Deck.

But most of the barriers were not down, and the steerage passengers who sensed danger and aimed for the boats were strictly on their own resources.

Like a stream of ants, a thin line of them curled their way up a crane in the after well deck, crawled along the boom to the First Class quarters, then over the railing and on up to the Boat Deck.

Some slipped under a rope that had been stretched across the after well deck, penning them even further to the stern than the regular barrier. But once through, it was fairly easy to get to the Second Class stairway and on up to the boats.

Others somehow reached the Second Class promenade space on B Deck, then couldn't find their way any further. In desperation they turned to an emergency ladder meant for the crew's use. This ladder was near the brightly lit windows of the First Class *à la carte* restaurant, and as Anna Sjoblom prepared to climb up with another girl, they looked in. They marveled at the tables beautifully set with silver and china for the following day. The other girl had an impulse to kick the window out and go inside, but Anna persuaded her that the company might make them pay for the damage.

Many of the steerage men climbed another emergency ladder from the forward well deck, and then up the regular First Class companionway to the boats.

Others beat on the barriers, demanding to be let through. As Third Class passenger Daniel Buckley climbed some steps leading to a gate to First Class, the man ahead of him was chucked down by a seaman standing guard. Furious, the passenger jumped to his feet and raced up the steps again. The seaman took one look, locked the gate and fled. The passenger smashed the lock and dashed through, howling what he would do if he caught the sailor. With the gate down, Buckley and dozens of others swarmed into First Class.

At another barrier a seaman held back Kathy Gilnagh, Kate Mullins and Kate Murphy. (On the *Titanic* all Irish girls seemed to be named Katherine.) Suddenly steerage passenger Jim Farrell, a strapping Irishman from the girls' home county, barged up. "Great God, man!" he roared. "Open the gate and let the girls through!" It was a superb demonstration of sheer voice-power. To the girls' astonishment the sailor meekly complied.

But for every steerage passenger who found a way up, hundreds milled aimlessly around the forward well deck . . . the after poop deck . . . or the foot of the E Deck staircase. Some holed up in their cabins—that's where Mary Agatha Glynn and four discouraged roommates were found by young Martin Gallagher. He quickly escorted them to Boat 13 and stepped back on the deck again. Others turned to prayer. When steerage passenger Gus Cohen passed the Third Class dining saloon about an hour after the crash, he saw quite a number gathered there, many with rosaries in their hands.

The staff of the First Class *à la carte* restaurant were having the hardest time of all. They were neither fish nor fowl. Obviously they weren't passengers, but technically they weren't crew either. The restaurant was not run by the White Star Line but by Monsieur Gatti as a concession.

Thus, the employees had no status at all. And to make matters worse, they were French and Italian—objects of deep Anglo-Saxon suspicion at a time like this in 1912.

From the very start they never had a chance. Steward Johnson remembered seeing them herded together down by their quarters on E Deck aft. Manager Gatti, his Chef and the Chef's Assistant, Paul Maugé, were the only ones who made it to the Boat Deck. They got through because they happened to be in civilian clothes; the crew thought they were passengers.

Down in the engine room no one even thought of getting away. Men struggled desperately to keep the steam up . . . the lights lit . . . the pumps going. Chief Engineer Bell had all the watertight doors raised aft of Boiler Room No. 4—when the water reached here they could be lowered again; meanwhile it would be easier to move around.

Greaser Fred Scott worked to free a shipmate trapped in the after tunnel behind one of the doors. Greaser Thomas Ranger turned off the last of the 45 ventilating fans—they used too much electricity. Trimmer Thomas Patrick Dillon helped drag long sections of pipe from the aft compartments, to get more volume out of the suction pump in boiler room No. 4.

Here, Trimmer George Cavell was busy drawing the fires. This meant even less power, but there must be no explosion when the sea reached No. 4. It was about 1:20 and the job was almost done when he noticed the water seeping up through the metal floor plates. Cavell worked faster. When it reached his knees, he had enough. He was almost at the top of the escape ladder when he began to feel he had quit on his mates. Down again, only to find they were gone too. His conscience clear, he climbed back up, this time for good.

Most of the boats were now gone. One by one they rowed slowly away from the *Titanic*, oars bumping and splashing in the glass-smooth sea.

"I never had an oar in my hand before, but I think I can row," a steward told Mrs. J. Stuart White, as No. 8 set out.

In every boat all eyes were glued on the *Titanic*. Her tall masts, the four big funnels stood out sharp and black in the clear blue night. The bright promenade decks, the long rows of portholes all blazed with light. From the boats they could see the people lining the rails; they could hear the ragtime in the still night air. It seemed impossible that anything could be wrong with this great ship; yet there they were out on the sea, and there she was, well down at the head. Brilliantly lit from stem to stern, she looked like a sagging birthday cake.

Clumsily the boats moved further away. Those told to stand by now lay on their oars. Others, told to make for the steamer whose lights shone in the distance, began their painful journey.

The steamer seemed agonizingly near. So near that Captain Smith told the people in Boat 8 to go over, land its passengers, and come back for more. About the same time he asked Quartermaster Rowe at the rocket gun if he could Morse. Rowe replied he could a little, and the Captain said, "Call that ship up and when she replies, tell us, 'We are the *Titanic* sinking; please have all your boats ready.' "

Boxhall had already tried to reach her, but Rowe was more than eager to try his own luck; so in between rocket firing he called her again and again. Still no answer. Then Rowe told Captain Smith he thought he saw another light on the starboard quarter. The old skipper squinted through his glasses, courteously told Rowe that it was a planet. But he liked the eagerness of his young Quartermaster, and he lent Rowe the glasses to see for himself.

Meanwhile Boxhall continued firing rockets. Sooner or later, somehow they would wake up the stranger.

On the bridge of the *Californian*, Second Officer Stone and Apprentice Gibson counted the rockets—five by 12:55. Gibson tried his Morse lamp again, and at one o'clock lifted his glasses for another look. He was just in time to see a sixth rocket.

At 1:10 Stone whistled down the speaking tube to the chart room and told Captain Lord. He called back, "Are they company signals?"

"I don't know," Stone answered, "but they appear to me to be white rockets.'"

The Captain advised him to go on Morsing.

A little later Stone handed his glasses to Gibson, remarking: "Have a look at her now. She looks very queer out of the water—her lights look queer."

Gibson studied the ship carefully. She seemed to be listing. She had, as he called it, "a big side out of the water." And Stone, standing beside him, noticed that her red side light had disappeared.

**Phillip Hoose**

# Justin Lebo

*Great acts of heroic kindness don't occur only in
life-and-death situations. Simply doing something for
someone in need can make one a hero.*

*Since he was ten, Justin Lebo, fourteen, of Paterson, New Jersey, has been
building bicycles out of used parts he finds from old junkers. When he fin-
ishes, he gives them away to kids who are homeless or sick. He plows most
of his allowance into the project and often works on nights and weekends.
Why does he do it? The answer is surprising. "In part," he says, "I do it for
myself."*

SOMETHING ABOUT THE BATTERED OLD BICYCLE at the
garage sale caught ten-year-old Justin Lebo's eye. What a wreck! It
was like looking at a few big bones in the dust and trying to figure out
what kind of dinosaur they had once belonged to.

It was a BMX bike with a twenty-inch frame. Its original color was
buried beneath five or six coats of gunky paint. Now it showed up as
sort of a rusted red. Everything—the grips, the pedals, the brakes, the
seat, the spokes—was bent or broken, twisted and rusted. Justin stood
back as if he were inspecting a painting for sale at an auction. Then
he made his final judgment: perfect.

Justin talked the owner down to $6.50 and asked his mother,
Diane, to help him load the bike into the back of their car.

When he got it home, he wheeled the junker into the garage and
showed it proudly to his father. "Will you help me fix it up?" he asked.
Justin's hobby was bike racing, a passion the two of them shared.
Their garage barely had room for the car anymore. It was more like a
bike shop. Tires and frames hung from hooks on the ceiling, and bike
wrenches dangled from the walls.

After every race, Justin and his father would adjust the brakes and realign the wheels of his two racing bikes. This was a lot of work, since Justin raced flat out, challenging every gear and part to perform to its fullest. He had learned to handle almost every repair his father could and maybe even a few things he couldn't. When Justin got really stuck, he went to see Mel, the owner of the best bike shop in town. Mel let him hang out and watch, and he even grunted a few syllables of advice from between the spokes of a wheel now and then.

Now Justin and his father cleared out a work space in the garage and put the old junker up on a rack. They poured alcohol on the frame and rubbed until the old paint began to yield, layer by layer. They replaced the broken pedal, tightened down a new seat, and restored the grips. In about a week, it looked brand new.

Justin wheeled it out of the garage, leapt aboard, and started off around the block. He stood up and mashed down on the pedals, straining for speed. It was a good, steady ride, but not much of a thrill compared to his racers.

Soon he forgot about the bike. But the very next week, he bought another junker at a yard sale and fixed it up, too. After a while it bothered him that he wasn't really using either bike. Then he realized that what he loved about the old bikes wasn't riding them: it was the challenge of making something new and useful out of something old and broken.

Justin wondered what he should do with them. They were just taking up space in the garage. He remembered that when he was younger, he used to live near a large brick building called the Kilbarchan Home for Boys. It was a place for boys whose parents couldn't care for them for one reason or another.

He found "Kilbarchan" in the phone book and called the director, who said the boys would be thrilled to get two bicycles. The next day when Justin and his mother unloaded the bikes at the home, two boys raced out to greet them. They leapt aboard the bikes and started tooling around the semicirular driveway, doing wheelies and pirouettes, laughing and shouting.

The Lebos watched them for a while, then started to climb into their car to go home. The boys cried after them, "Wait a minute! You forgot your bikes!" Justin explained that the bikes were for them to keep. "They were so happy," Justin remembers. "It was like they couldn't believe it. It made me feel good just to see them happy."

On the way home, Justin was silent. His mother assumed he was lost in a feeling of satisfaction. But he was thinking about what would happen once those bikes got wheeled inside and everyone saw them. How would all those kids decide who got the bikes? Two bikes could cause more trouble than they would solve. Actually, they hadn't been that hard to build. It was fun. Maybe he could do more. . . .

"Mom," Justin said as they turned onto their street, "I've got an idea. I'm going to make a bike for every boy at Kilbarchan for Christmas." Diane Lebo looked at Justin out of the corner of her eye. She had rarely seen him so determined.

When they got home, Justin called Kilbarchan to find out how many boys lived there. There were twenty-one. It was already June. He had six months to make nineteen bikes. That was almost a bike a week. Justin called the home back to tell them of his plan. "I could tell they didn't think I could do it," Justin remembers. "I knew I could."

## "It Just Snowballed."

Justin knew his best chance was to build bikes almost the way GM or Ford builds cars: in an assembly line. He would start with frames from three-speed, twenty-four-inch BMX bicycles. They were common bikes, and all the parts were interchangeable. If he could find enough decent frames, he could take parts off broken bikes and fasten them onto the good frames. He figured it would take three or four junkers to produce enough parts to make one good bike. That meant sixty to eighty bikes. Where would he get them?

Garage sales seemed to be the only hope. It was June, and there would be garage sales all summer long. But even if he could find that many bikes, how could he ever pay for them? That was hundreds of dollars.

He went to his parents with a proposal. "When Justin was younger, say five or six," says his mother, "he used to give some of his allowance away to help others in need. His father and I would donate a dollar for every dollar Justin donated. So he asked us if it could be like the old days, if we'd match every dollar he put into buying old bikes. We said yes."

Justin and his mother spent most of June and July hunting for cheap bikes at garage sales and thrift shops. They would haul the bikes home, and Justin would start stripping them down in the yard.

But by the beginning of August, he had managed to make only ten bikes. Summer vacation was almost over, and school and homework would soon cut into his time. Garage sales would dry up when it got colder, and Justin was out of money. Still, he was determined to find a way.

At the end of August, Justin got a break. A neighbor wrote a letter to the local newspaper describing Justin's project, and an editor thought it would make a good story. One day a reporter entered the Lebo garage. Stepping gingerly through the tires and frames that covered the floor, she found a boy with cut fingers and dirty nails, banging a seat onto a frame. His clothes were covered with grease. In her admiring article about a boy who was devoting his summer to help kids he didn't even know, she said Justin needed bikes and money, and she printed his home phone number.

Overnight, everything changed. "There must have been a hundred calls," Justin says. "People would call me up and ask me to come over and pick up their old bike. Or I'd be working in the garage, and a station wagon would pull up. The driver would leave a couple of bikes by the curb. It just snowballed."

By the start of school, the garage was overflowing with BMX frames. Pyramids of pedals and seats rose in the corners. Soon bike parts filled a toolshed in the backyard and then spilled out into the small yard itself, wearing away the lawn.

More and more writers and television and radio reporters called for interviews. Each time he told his story, Justin asked for bikes and money. "The first few interviews were fun," Justin says, "but it reached a point where I really didn't like doing them. The publicity was necessary, though. I had to keep doing interviews to get the donations I needed."

By the time school opened, he was working on ten bikes at a time. There were so many calls now that he was beginning to refuse offers that weren't the exact bikes he needed.

As checks came pouring in, Justin's money problems disappeared. He set up a bank account and began to make bulk orders of common parts from Mel's bike shop. Mel seemed delighted to see him. Sometimes, if Justin brought a bike by the shop, Mel would help him fix it. When Justin tried to talk him into a lower price for big orders, Mel smiled and gave in. He respected another good businessman. They became friends.

## "Why Do You Do It?"

The week before Christmas Justin delivered the last of the twenty-one bikes to Kilbarchan. Once again, the boys poured out of the home and leapt aboard the bikes, tearing around the snow.

And once again, their joy inspired Justin. They reminded him how important bikes were to him. Wheels meant freedom. He thought how much more the freedom to ride must mean to boys like these who had so little freedom in their lives. He decided to keep on building.

"First I made eleven bikes for the children in a foster home my mother told me about. Then I made bikes for all the women in a battered women's shelter. Then I made ten little bikes and tricycles for the kids in a home for children with AIDS. Then I made twenty-three bikes for the Paterson Housing Coalition."

In the four years since he started, Justin Lebo has made between 150 and 200 bikes and given them all away. He has been careful to leave time for his homework, his friends, his coin collection, his new interest in marine biology, and of course his own bikes.

Reporters and interviewers have asked Justin Lebo the same question over and over: "Why do you do it?" The question seems to make him uncomfortable. It's as if they want him to say what a great person he is. Their stories always make him seem like a saint, which he knows he isn't. "Sure it's nice of me to make the bikes," he says, "because I don't have to. But I want to. In part, I do it for myself. I don't think you can ever really do anything to help anybody else if it doesn't make you happy.

"Once I overheard a kid who got one of my bikes say, 'A bike is like a book; it opens up a whole new world.' That's how I feel, too. It made me happy to know that kid felt that way. That's why I do it."

**Robert Frost**

# A Time to Talk

*Sometimes the best way to touch another person's
life is simply to take time out of a busy day for
a little talk.*

When a friend calls to me from the road
And slows his horse to a meaning walk,
I don't stand still and look around
On all the hills I haven't hoed,
5   And shout from where I am, What is it?
No, not as there is a time to talk.
I thrust my hoe in the mellow ground,
Blade-end up and five feet tall,
And plod: I go up to the stone wall
10   For a friendly visit.

Rich Johnson,
ABC News,
Darien

# Teen Run ER

*In an emergency situation when lives are in danger,
the age of the rescuers is not important. All that
matters is their ability and their determination
to save lives.*

W HILE MOST HIGH SCHOOL KIDS are worryng about what to wear to the dance on Saturday night, or how to find time to study for their mid-terms, some kids in Darien, Connecticut, have committed themselves to some heavier responsibilities. The staff of the town's ambulance crew is made up of a group of very special teenagers. Here's a look at these extraordinary high-schoolers that use their spare time to save lives.

Imagine you've been in an accident, or let's say someone you love has had a heart attack. You call 911, an ambulance arrives, and out rush . . . teenagers. If you get sick or hurt in Darien, Connecticut, that's just what happens. Post 53, the ambulance service for this town of about 20,000 residents, is staffed exclusively by high-schoolers aged 14 to 18.

Tricia Rogers is the student president of Post 53, she says her age sometimes gets a reaction: "I've had a couple of people ask me 'how old are you.' I just say 'I'm 16 years old and I'm in high school' and you do get some strange looks."

The program in Darien started in 1970, and has continued to this day, with over 600 students participating in the program over the years. Connecticut is the only state with no age requirement for EMT certification, so kids as young as 14 can—and do—answer ambulance calls.

An adult supervisor always rides to the scene with the teenagers, but generally stays in the background. "Most of the time when people are in dire need, they don't really judge who's there, it's just 'help me right now,' says Marilyn Vojta, Post 53 Adult Supervisor who's volunteered in this position for 15 years.

Vojta rides in a separate car to the scene and stands by in case a victim needs an IV or defibrillation—some of the only procedures the kids are not allowed to perform. The kids are responsible for every aspect of the program, from fundraising, to training young incoming members. It's a job they take very seriously, and responsibility of it breeds strong friendships.

"The bond we have is unbelievable. I mean we share these experiences, we see death and you're with only four other kids and an adult. That's a really close bond," says teen participant Rogers.

And though they act like the teenagers when they are relaxing, after watching them at work, it's obvious these kids are pros. "They're kids when they're down here, they goof around and they laugh, do their homework, talk on the phone, but it's amazing how mature they get when they step on that ambulance. They have the ability to rise to the occasion and do an excellent job," summarizes Vojta.

# Too Soon a Woman

**Dorothy M. Johnson**

*A person's true character can sometimes be seen most clearly in life-and-death situations.*

WE LEFT THE HOME PLACE BEHIND, mile by slow mile, heading for the mountains, across the prairie where the wind blew forever.

At first there were four of us with the one-horse wagon and its skimpy load. Pa and I walked, because I was a big boy of eleven. My two little sisters romped and trotted until they got tired and had to be boosted up into the wagon bed.

That was no covered Conestoga, like Pa's folks came west in, but just an old farm wagon, drawn by one weary horse, creaking and rumbling westward to the mountains, toward the little woods town where Pa thought he had an old uncle who owned a little two-bit sawmill.

Two weeks we had been moving when we picked up Mary, who had run away from somewhere that she wouldn't tell. Pa didn't want her along, but she stood up to him with no fear in her voice.

"I'd rather go with a family and look after the kids," she said, "but I ain't going back. If you won't take me, I'll travel with any wagon that will."

Pa scowled at her, and her wide blue eyes stared back.

"How old are you?" he demanded.

"Eighteen," she said. "There's teamsters come this way sometimes. I'd rather go with you folks. But I won't go back."

"We're prid'near out of grub," my father told her. "We're clean out of money. I got all I can handle without taking anybody else." He turned away as if he hated the sight of her. "You'll have to walk," he said.

So she went along with us and looked after the little girls, but Pa wouldn't talk to her.

On the prairie, the wind blew. But in the mountains, there was rain. When we stopped at little timber claims along the way, the homesteaders said it had rained all summer. Crops among the blackened stumps were rotted and spoiled. There was no cheer anywhere and little hospitality. The people we talked to were past worrying. They were scared and desperate.

So was Pa. He traveled twice as far each day as the wagon. He ranged through the woods with his rifle, but he never saw game. He had been depending on venison, but we never got any except as a grudging gift from the homesteaders.

He brought in a porcupine once; that was fat meat and good. Mary roasted it in chunks over the fire, half crying with the smoke. Pa and I rigged up the tarp sheet for a shelter to keep the rain from putting the fire clean out.

The porcupine was long gone, except for some of the dried-out fat that Mary had saved, when we came to an old, empty cabin. Pa said we'd have to stop. The horse was wore out, couldn't pull anymore up those grades on the deep-rutted roads in the mountains.

At the cabin, at least there was shelter. We had a few potatoes left and some corn meal. There was a creek that probably had fish in it, if a person could catch them. Pa tried it for half a day before he gave up. To this day I don't care for fishing. I remember my father's sunken eyes in his gaunt, grim face.

He took Mary and me outside the cabin to talk. Rain dripped on us from branches overhead.

"I think I know where we are," he said. "I calculate to get to old John's and back in about four days. There'll be grub in the town, and they'll let me have some whether old John's still there or not."

He looked at me. "You do like she tells you," he warned. It was the first time he had admitted Mary was on earth since we picked her up two weeks before.

"You're my pardner," he said to me, "but it might be she's got more brains. You mind what she says."

He burst out with bitterness, "There ain't anything good left in the world, or people to care if you live or die. But I'll get grub in the town and come back with it."

He took a deep breath and added, "If you get too all-fired hungry, butcher the horse. It'll be better than starvin'."

He kissed the little girls good-bye and plodded off through the woods with one blanket and the rifle.

The cabin was moldy and had no floor. We kept a fire going under a hole in the roof, so it was full of blinding smoke, but we had to keep the fire so as to dry out the wood.

The third night, we lost the horse. A bear scared him. We heard the racket, and Mary and I ran out, but we couldn't see anything in the pitch dark.

In gray daylight I went looking for him, and I must have walked fifteen miles. It seemed like I had to have that horse at the cabin when Pa came or he'd whip me. I got plumb lost two or three times and thought maybe I was going to die there alone and nobody would ever know it, but I found the way back to the clearing.

That was the fourth day, and Pa didn't come. That was the day we ate up the last of the grub.

The fifth day, Mary went looking for the horse. My sisters whimpered, huddled in a quilt by the fire, because they were scared and hungry.

I never did get dried out, always having to bring in more damp wood and going out to yell to see if Mary would hear me and not get lost. But I couldn't cry like the little girls did, because I was a big boy, eleven years old.

It was near dark when there was an answer to my yelling, and Mary came into the clearing.

Mary didn't have the horse—we never saw hide nor hair of that old horse again—but she was carrying something big and white that looked like a pumpkin with no color to it.

She didn't say anything, just looked around and saw Pa wasn't there yet, at the end of the fifth day.

"What's that thing?" my sister Elizabeth demanded.

"Mushroom," Mary answered. "I bet it hefts ten pounds."

"What are you going to do with it now?" I sneered. "Play football here?"

"Eat it—maybe," she said, putting it in a corner. Her wet hair hung over her shoulders. She huddled by the fire.

My sister Sarah began to whimper again. "I'm hungry!" she kept saying.

"Mushrooms ain't good eating," I said. "They can kill you."

"Maybe," Mary answered. "Maybe they can. I don't set up to know all about everything, like some people."

"What's that mark on your shoulder?" I asked her. "You tore your dress on the brush."

"What do you think it is?" she said, her head bowed in the smoke.

"Looks like scars," I guessed.

"'Tis scars. They whipped me. Now mind your own business. I want to think."

Elizabeth whimpered, "Why don't Pa come back?"

"He's coming," Mary promised. "Can't come in the dark. Your pa'll take care of you soon's he can."

She got up and rummaged around in the grub box.

"Nothing there but empty dishes," I growled. "If there was anything, we'd know it."

Mary stood up. She was holding the can with the porcupine grease.

"I'm going to have something to eat," she said coolly. "You kids can't have any yet. And I don't want any squalling, mind."

It was a cruel thing, what she did then. She sliced that big, solid mushroom and heated grease in a pan.

The smell of it brought the little girls out of their quilt, but she told them to go back in so fierce a voice that they obeyed. They cried to break your heart.

I didn't cry. I watched, hating her.

I endured the smell of the mushroom frying as long as I could. Then I said, "Give me some."

"Tomorrow," Mary answered. "Tomorrow, maybe. But not tonight." She turned to me with a sharp command: "Don't bother me! Just leave me be."

She knelt there by the fire and finished frying the slice of mushroom.

If I'd had Pa's rifle, I'd have been willing to kill her right then and there.

She didn't eat right away. She looked at the brown, fried slice for a while and said, "By tomorrow morning, I guess you can tell whether you want any."

The little girls stared at her as she ate. Sarah was chewing an old leather glove.

When Mary crawled into the quilts with them, they moved away as far as they could get.

I was so scared that my stomach heaved, empty as it was.

Mary didn't stay in the quilts long. She took a drink out of the water bucket and sat down by the fire and looked through the smoke at me.

She said in a low voice, "I don't know how it will be if it's poison. Just do the best you can with the girls. Because your pa will come back, you know. . . . You better go to bed, I'm going to sit up."

And so would you sit up. If it might be your last night on earth and the pain of death might seize you at any moment, you would sit up by the smoky fire, wide-awake, remembering whatever you had to remember, savoring life.

We sat in silence after the girls had gone to sleep. Once I asked, "How long does it take?"

"I never heard," she answered. "Don't think about it."

I slept after a while, with my chin on my chest. Maybe Peter dozed that way at Gethsemane as the Lord knelt praying.

Mary's moving around brought me wide-awake. The black of night was fading.

"I guess it's all right," Mary said. "I'd be able to tell by now, wouldn't I?"

I answered gruffly, "I don't know."

Mary stood in the doorway for a while, looking out at the dripping world as if she found it beautiful. Then she fried slices of the mushroom while the little girls danced with anxiety.

We feasted, we three, my sisters and I, until Mary ruled, "That'll hold you," and would not cook any more. She didn't touch any of the mushroom herself.

That was a strange day in the moldy cabin. Mary laughed and was gay; she told stories, and we played "Who's Got the Thimble?" with a pine cone.

In the afternoon we heard a shout, and my sisters screamed, and I ran ahead of them across the clearing.

The rain had stopped. My father came plunging out of the woods leading a packhorse—and well I remember the treasures of food in that pack.

He glanced at us anxiously as he tore at the ropes that bound the pack.

"Where's the other one?" he demanded.

Mary came out of the cabin then, walking sedately. As she came toward us, the sun began to shine.

My stepmother was a wonderful woman.